REBELLION

Creative Director and CEO: Jason Kingsley
Chief Technical Officer: Chris Kingsley
Head of Books & Comics: Ben Smith
Roy of the Rovers Brand Manager: Rob Power
Roy of the Rovers Editor: Keith Richardson
Graphic Design: Sam Gretton

Published by Rebellion,
Riverside House, Osney Mead, Oxford, OX2 0ES, UK.
www.rebellionpublishing.co.uk

Manufactured in Ukraine by Imago.

First Printing: November 2018
10 9 8 7 6 5 4 3 2 1

www.royoftheroversofficial.com
 royoftheroversofficial 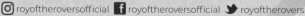 royoftheroversofficial royoftherovers

ROY OF THE ROVERS™

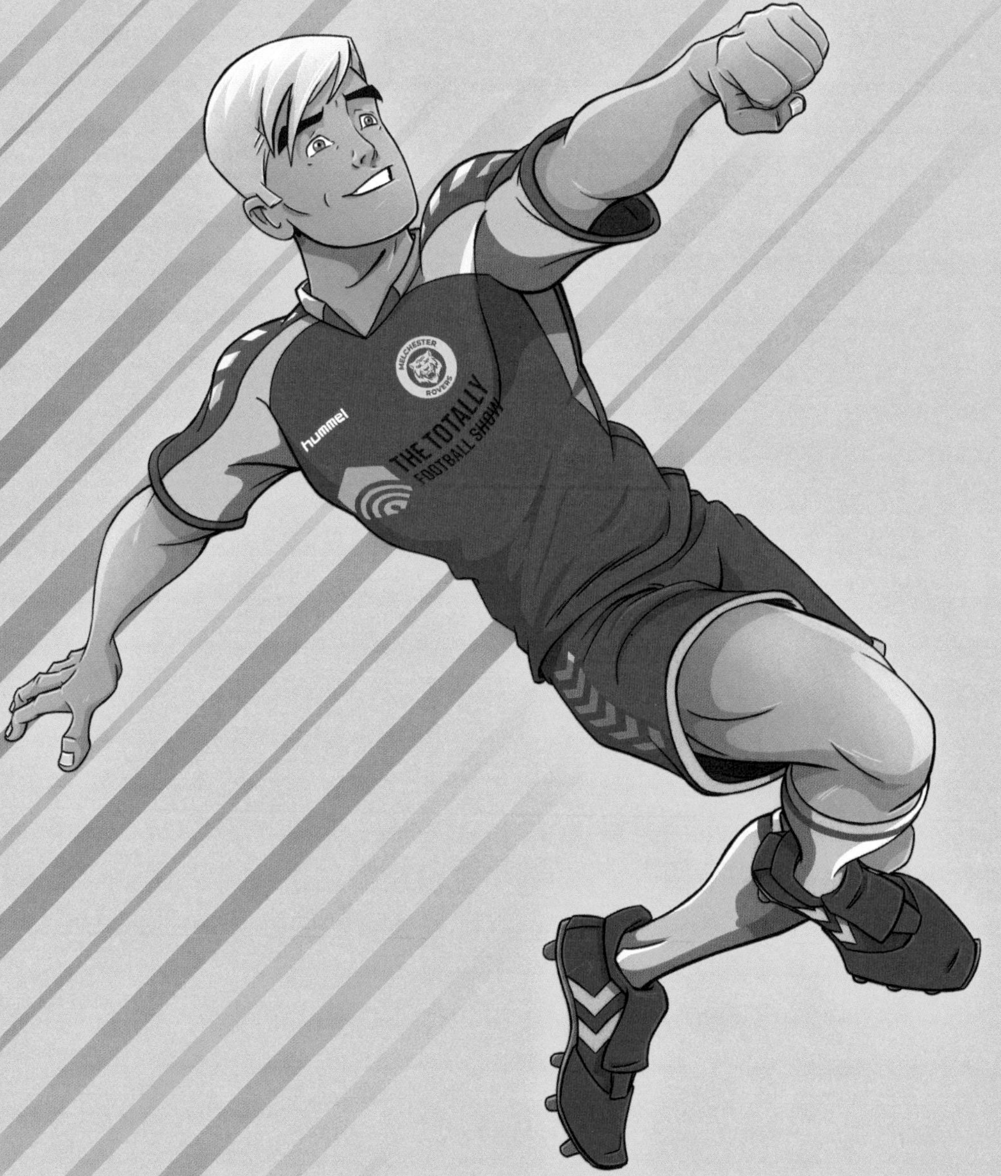
MELCHESTER ROVERS
hummel
THE TOTALLY FOOTBALL SHOW

KICK-OFF

ROB **WILLIAMS** BEN **WILLSHER**

B O O K O N E
KICK-OFF

Script
ROB WILLIAMS

Art
BEN WILLSHER

Letters
JIM CAMPBELL

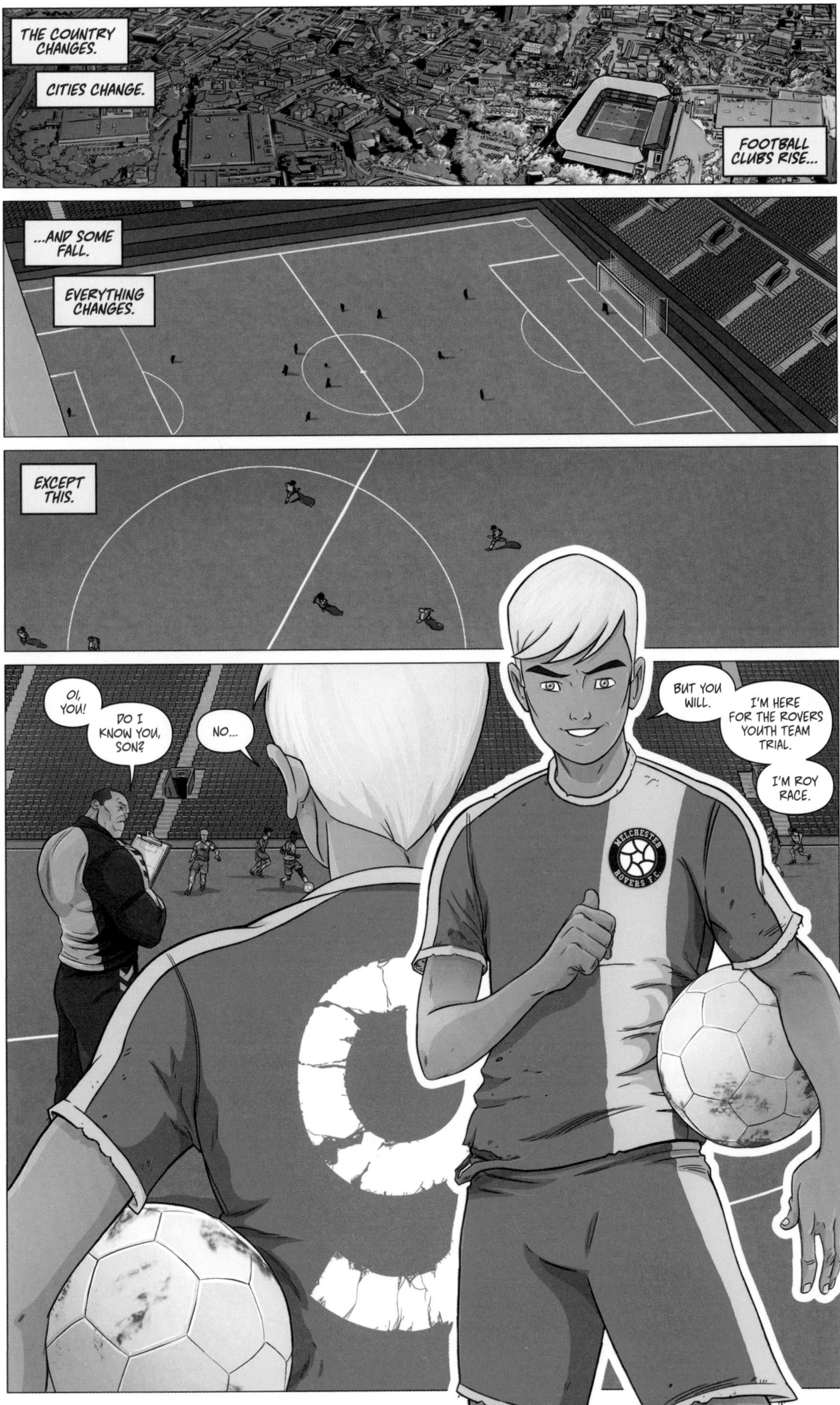
THE COUNTRY CHANGES.
CITIES CHANGE.
FOOTBALL CLUBS RISE...
...AND SOME FALL.
EVERYTHING CHANGES.
EXCEPT THIS.
OI, YOU!
DO I KNOW YOU, SON?
NO...
BUT YOU WILL.
I'M HERE FOR THE ROVERS YOUTH TEAM TRIAL.
I'M ROY RACE.
MELCHESTER ROVERS F.C.

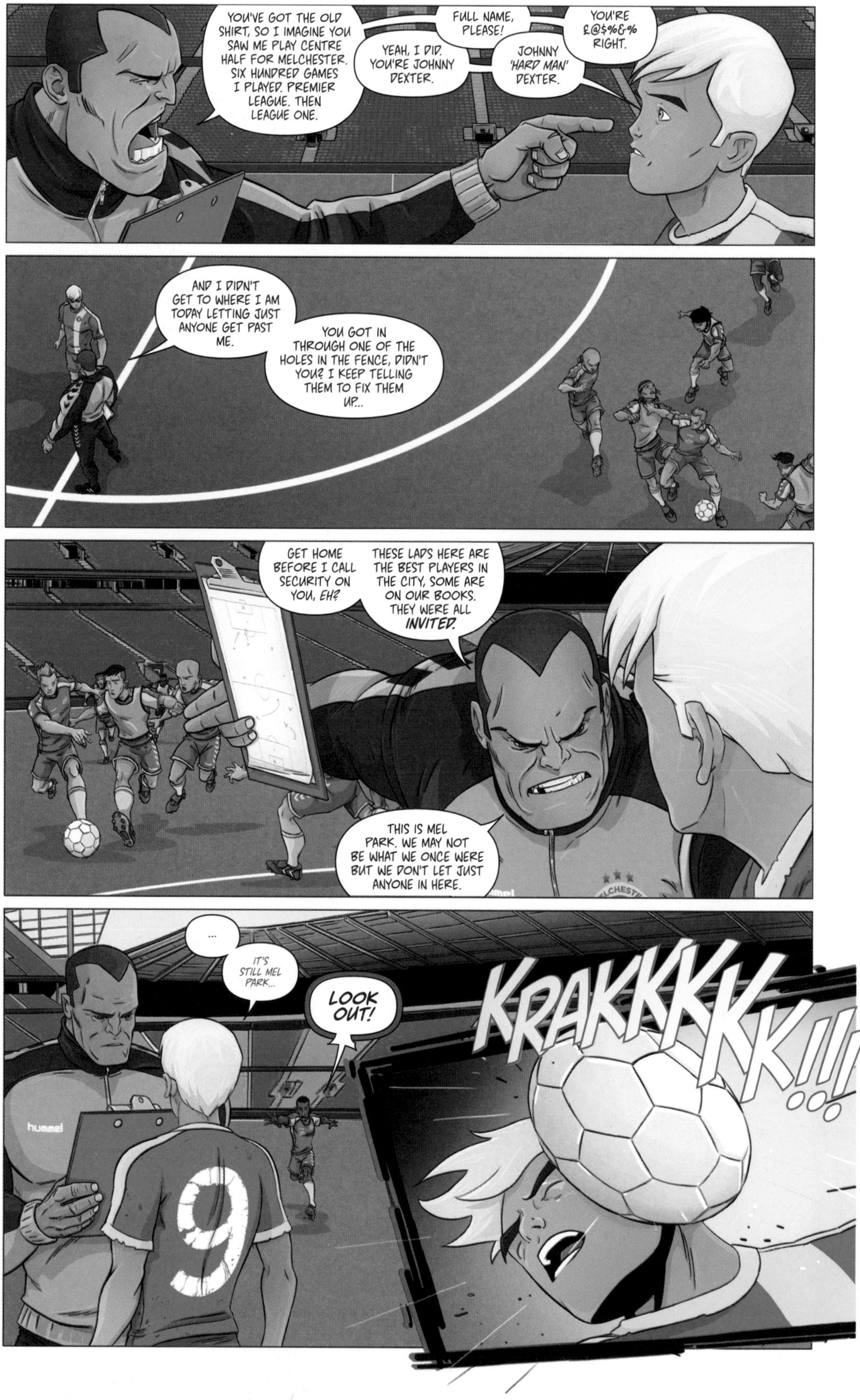
YOU'VE GOT THE OLD SHIRT, SO I IMAGINE YOU SAW ME PLAY CENTRE HALF FOR MELCHESTER. SIX HUNDRED GAMES I PLAYED. PREMIER LEAGUE. THEN LEAGUE ONE.
YEAH, I DID. YOU'RE JOHNNY DEXTER.
FULL NAME, PLEASE!
JOHNNY 'HARD MAN' DEXTER.
YOU'RE £@$%&% RIGHT.
AND I DIDN'T GET TO WHERE I AM TODAY LETTING JUST ANYONE GET PAST ME.
YOU GOT IN THROUGH ONE OF THE HOLES IN THE FENCE, DIDN'T YOU? I KEEP TELLING THEM TO FIX THEM UP...
GET HOME BEFORE I CALL SECURITY ON YOU, EH?
THESE LADS HERE ARE THE BEST PLAYERS IN THE CITY, SOME ARE ON OUR BOOKS. THEY WERE ALL INVITED.
THIS IS MEL PARK. WE MAY NOT BE WHAT WE ONCE WERE BUT WE DON'T LET JUST ANYONE IN HERE.
...
IT'S STILL MEL PARK...
LOOK OUT!
KRAKKKKK!!!

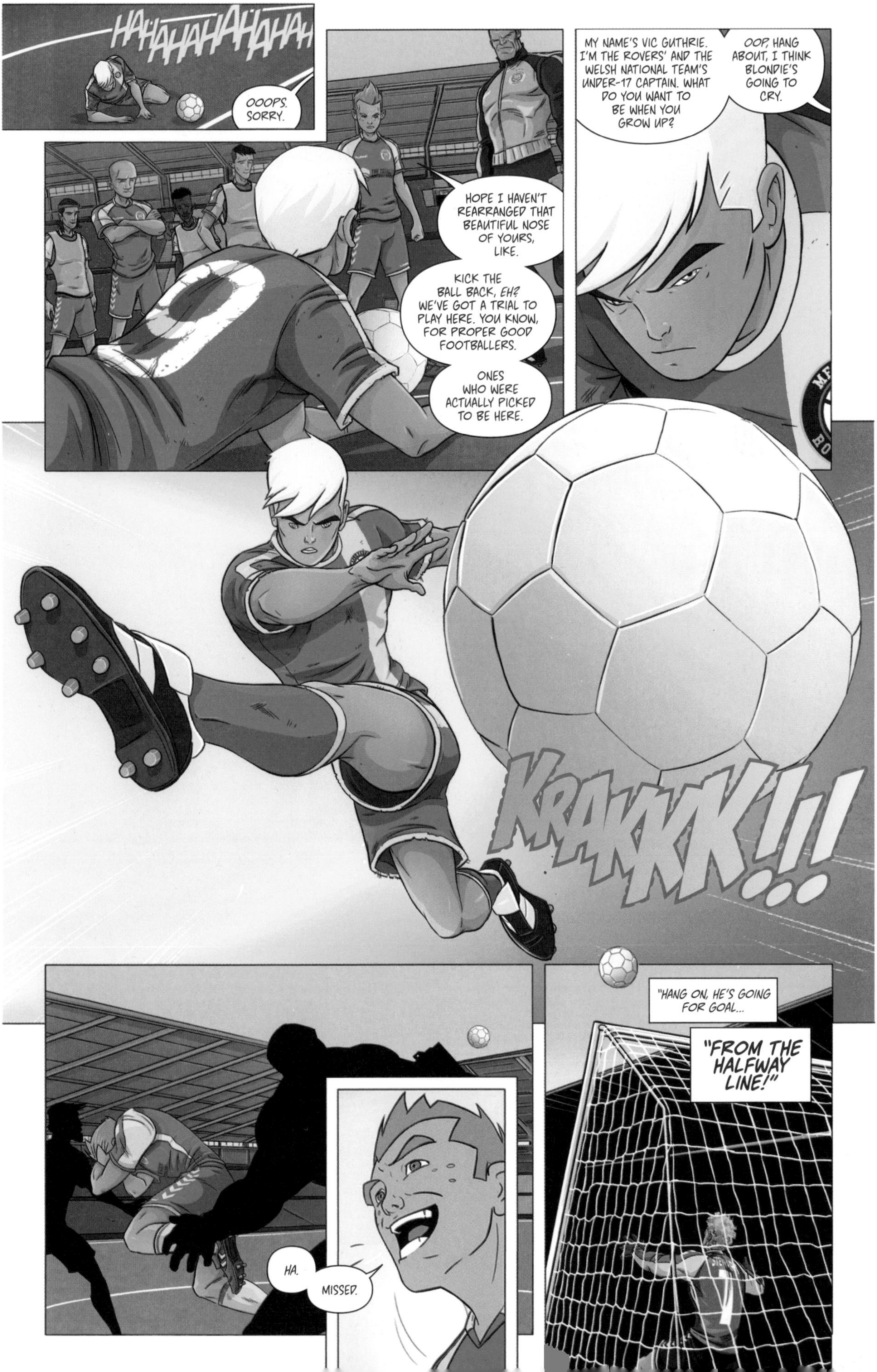
HAHAHAHAHAHAHAH
OOOPS. SORRY.
HOPE I HAVEN'T REARRANGED THAT BEAUTIFUL NOSE OF YOURS, LIKE.
KICK THE BALL BACK, *EH?* WE'VE GOT A TRIAL TO PLAY HERE. YOU KNOW, FOR PROPER GOOD FOOTBALLERS.
ONES WHO WERE ACTUALLY PICKED TO BE HERE.
MY NAME'S VIC GUTHRIE. I'M THE ROVERS' AND THE WELSH NATIONAL TEAM'S UNDER-17 CAPTAIN. WHAT DO YOU WANT TO BE WHEN YOU GROW UP?
OOP, HANG ABOUT, I THINK BLONDIE'S GOING TO CRY.
KRAKKK!!!
HA.
MISSED.
"HANG ON, HE'S GOING FOR GOAL...
"FROM THE HALFWAY LINE!"

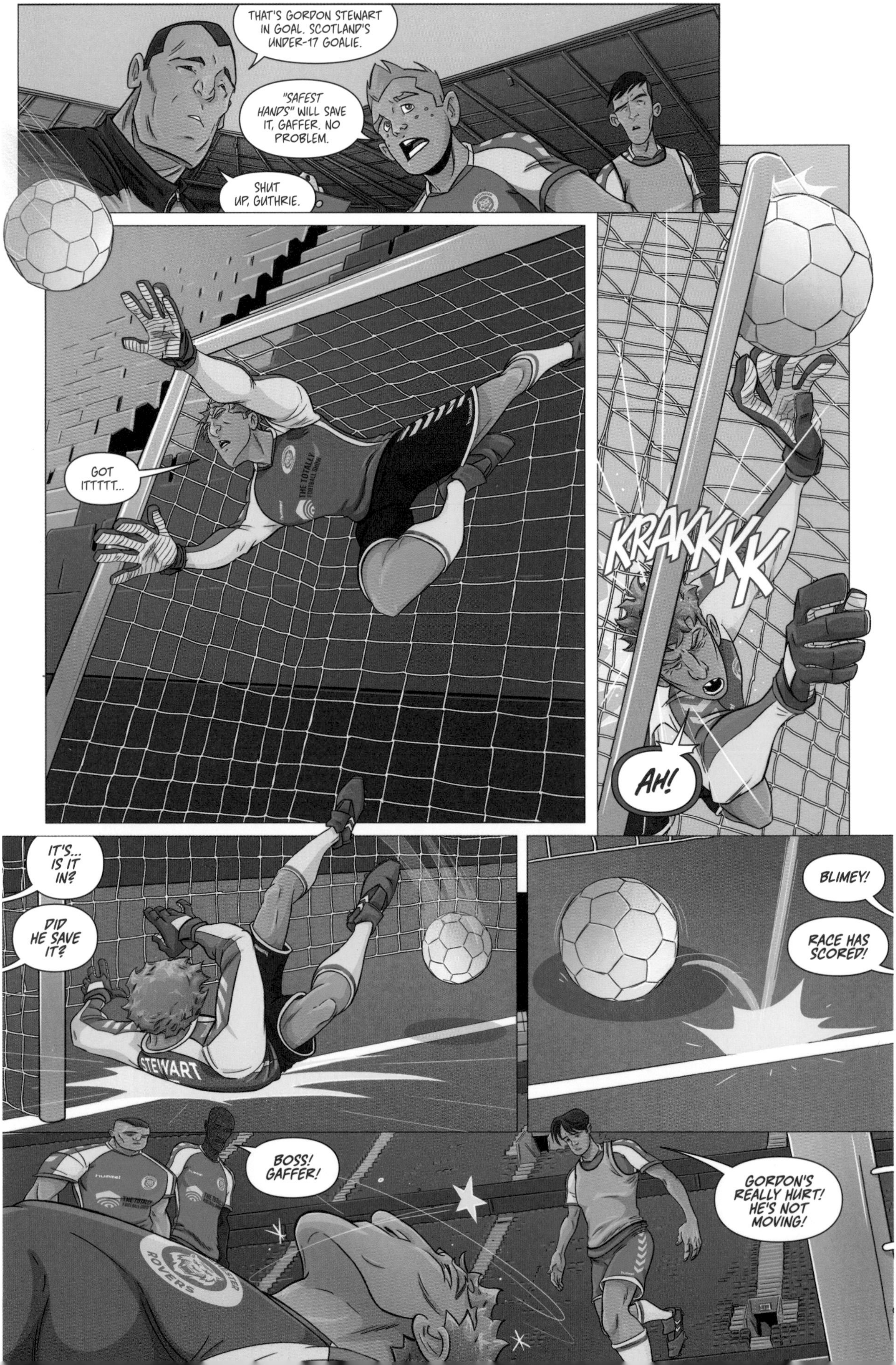
THAT'S GORDON STEWART IN GOAL. SCOTLAND'S UNDER-17 GOALIE.
"SAFEST HANDS" WILL SAVE IT, GAFFER. NO PROBLEM.
SHUT UP, GUTHRIE.
GOT ITTTTT...
KRAKKKK
AH!
IT'S... IS IT IN?
DID HE SAVE IT?
STEWART
BLIMEY!
RACE HAS SCORED!
BOSS! GAFFER!
GORDON'S REALLY HURT! HE'S NOT MOVING!

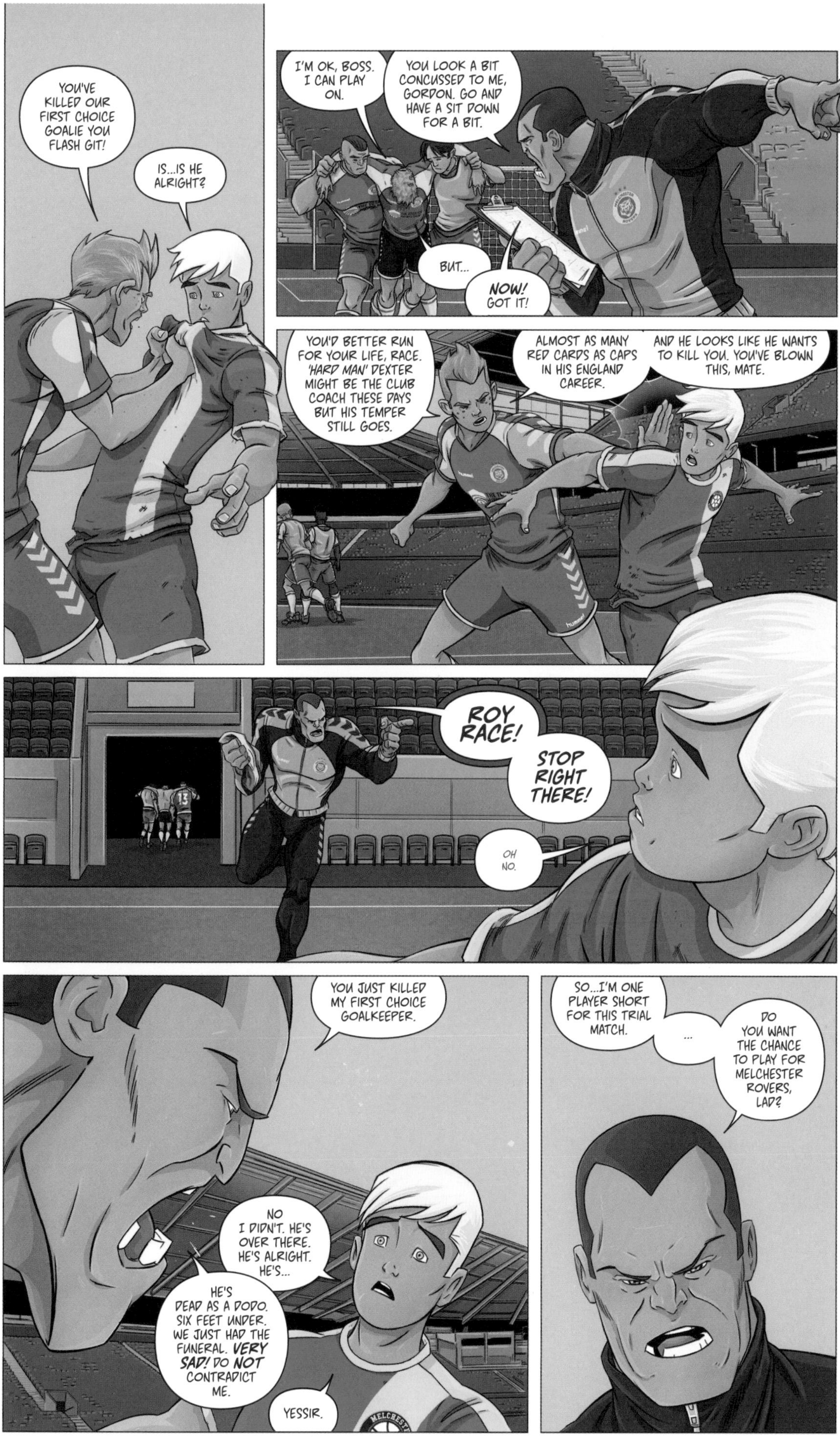
YOU'VE KILLED OUR FIRST CHOICE GOALIE YOU FLASH GIT!
IS...IS HE ALRIGHT?
I'M OK, BOSS. I CAN PLAY ON.
YOU LOOK A BIT CONCUSSED TO ME, GORDON. GO AND HAVE A SIT DOWN FOR A BIT.
BUT...
NOW! GOT IT!
YOU'D BETTER RUN FOR YOUR LIFE, RACE. 'HARD MAN' DEXTER MIGHT BE THE CLUB COACH THESE DAYS BUT HIS TEMPER STILL GOES.
ALMOST AS MANY RED CARDS AS CAPS IN HIS ENGLAND CAREER.
AND HE LOOKS LIKE HE WANTS TO KILL YOU. YOU'VE BLOWN THIS, MATE.
ROY RACE!
STOP RIGHT THERE!
OH NO.
YOU JUST KILLED MY FIRST CHOICE GOALKEEPER.
NO I DIDN'T. HE'S OVER THERE. HE'S ALRIGHT. HE'S...
HE'S DEAD AS A DODO. SIX FEET UNDER. WE JUST HAD THE FUNERAL. VERY SAD! DO NOT CONTRADICT ME.
YESSIR.
SO...I'M ONE PLAYER SHORT FOR THIS TRIAL MATCH.
...
DO YOU WANT THE CHANCE TO PLAY FOR MELCHESTER ROVERS, LAD?

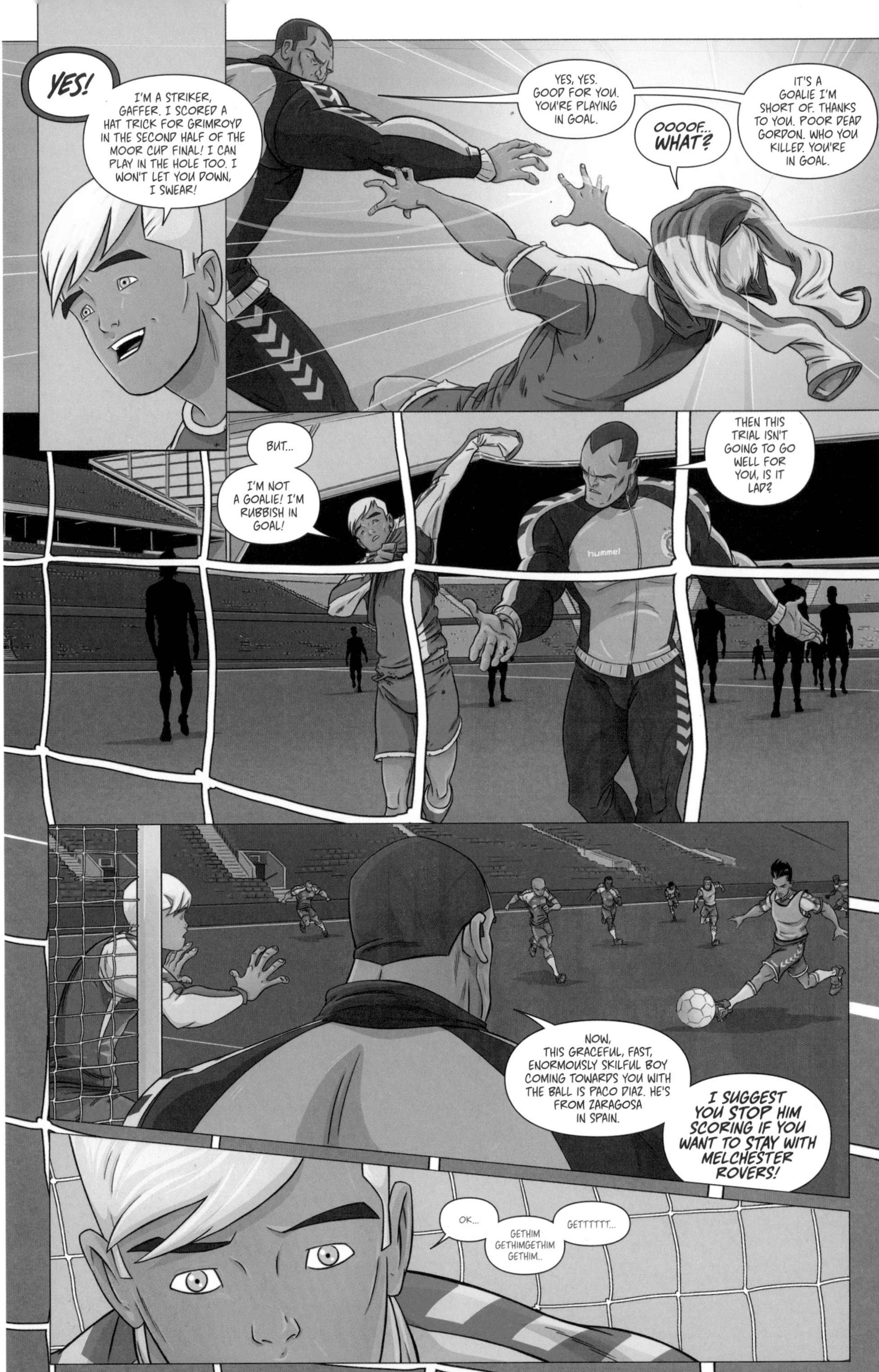
YES!
I'M A STRIKER, GAFFER. I SCORED A HAT TRICK FOR GRIMROYD IN THE SECOND HALF OF THE MOOR CUP FINAL! I CAN PLAY IN THE HOLE TOO. I WON'T LET YOU DOWN, I SWEAR!
YES, YES. GOOD FOR YOU. YOU'RE PLAYING IN GOAL.
OOOOF... WHAT?
IT'S A GOALIE I'M SHORT OF. THANKS TO YOU. POOR DEAD GORDON. WHO YOU KILLED. YOU'RE IN GOAL.
BUT...
I'M NOT A GOALIE! I'M RUBBISH IN GOAL!
THEN THIS TRIAL ISN'T GOING TO GO WELL FOR YOU, IS IT LAD?
hummel
NOW, THIS GRACEFUL, FAST, ENORMOUSLY SKILFUL BOY COMING TOWARDS YOU WITH THE BALL IS PACO DIAZ. HE'S FROM ZARAGOSA IN SPAIN.
I SUGGEST YOU STOP HIM SCORING IF YOU WANT TO STAY WITH MELCHESTER ROVERS!
OK...
GETHIM GETHIMGETHIM GETHIM..
GETTTTTT...

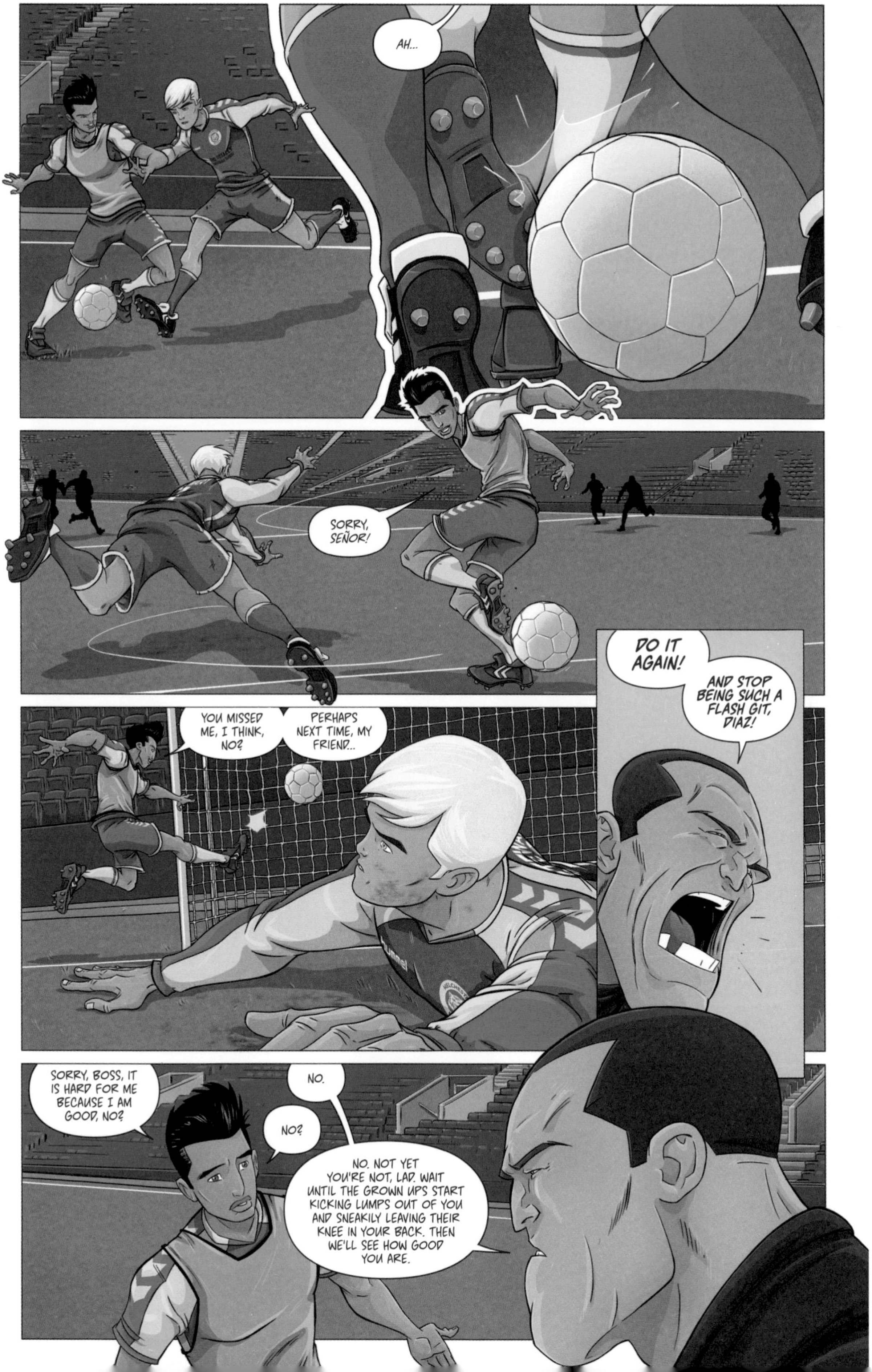
AH...
SORRY, SEÑOR!
YOU MISSED ME, I THINK, NO?
PERHAPS NEXT TIME, MY FRIEND...
DO IT AGAIN!
AND STOP BEING SUCH A FLASH GIT, DIAZ!
SORRY, BOSS, IT IS HARD FOR ME BECAUSE I AM GOOD, NO?
NO.
NO?
NO. NOT YET YOU'RE NOT, LAD. WAIT UNTIL THE GROWN UPS START KICKING LUMPS OUT OF YOU AND SNEAKILY LEAVING THEIR KNEE IN YOUR BACK. THEN WE'LL SEE HOW GOOD YOU ARE.

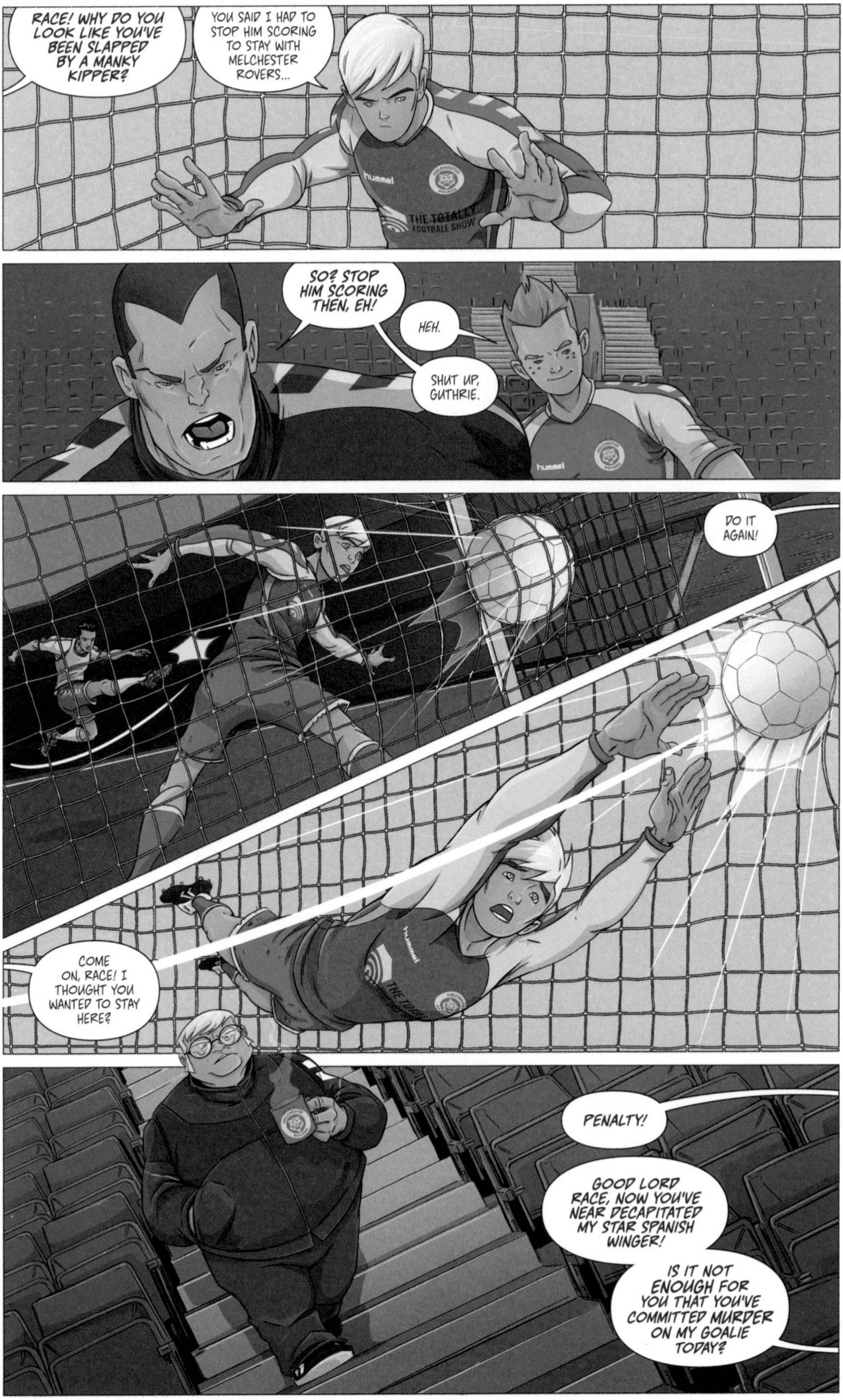
RACE! WHY DO YOU LOOK LIKE YOU'VE BEEN SLAPPED BY A MANKY KIPPER?
YOU SAID I HAD TO STOP HIM SCORING TO STAY WITH MELCHESTER ROVERS...
hummel
THE TOTALLY FOOTBALL SHOW
SO? STOP HIM SCORING THEN, EH!
HEH.
SHUT UP, GUTHRIE.
hummel
DO IT AGAIN!
COME ON, RACE! I THOUGHT YOU WANTED TO STAY HERE?
hummel
PENALTY!
GOOD LORD RACE, NOW YOU'VE NEAR DECAPITATED MY STAR SPANISH WINGER!
IS IT NOT ENOUGH FOR YOU THAT YOU'VE COMMITTED MURDER ON MY GOALIE TODAY?

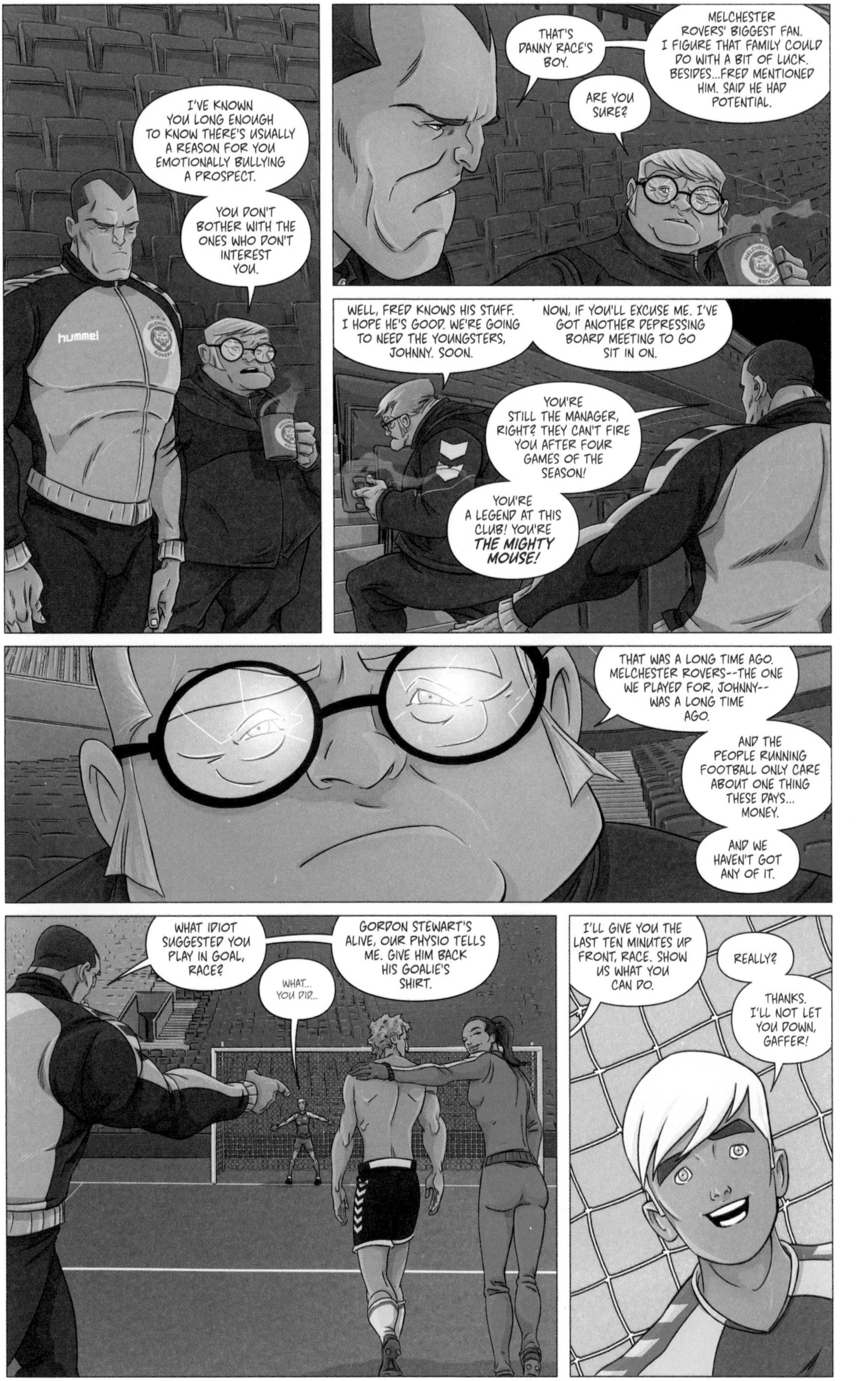

I'VE KNOWN YOU LONG ENOUGH TO KNOW THERE'S USUALLY A REASON FOR YOU EMOTIONALLY BULLYING A PROSPECT.
YOU DON'T BOTHER WITH THE ONES WHO DON'T INTEREST YOU.
hummel
THAT'S DANNY RACE'S BOY.
MELCHESTER ROVERS' BIGGEST FAN. I FIGURE THAT FAMILY COULD DO WITH A BIT OF LUCK. BESIDES...FRED MENTIONED HIM. SAID HE HAD POTENTIAL.
ARE YOU SURE?
WELL, FRED KNOWS HIS STUFF. I HOPE HE'S GOOD. WE'RE GOING TO NEED THE YOUNGSTERS, JOHNNY. SOON.
NOW, IF YOU'LL EXCUSE ME. I'VE GOT ANOTHER DEPRESSING BOARD MEETING TO GO SIT IN ON.
YOU'RE STILL THE MANAGER, RIGHT? THEY CAN'T FIRE YOU AFTER FOUR GAMES OF THE SEASON!
YOU'RE A LEGEND AT THIS CLUB! YOU'RE ***THE MIGHTY MOUSE!***
THAT WAS A LONG TIME AGO. MELCHESTER ROVERS--THE ONE WE PLAYED FOR, JOHNNY--WAS A LONG TIME AGO.
AND THE PEOPLE RUNNING FOOTBALL ONLY CARE ABOUT ONE THING THESE DAYS... MONEY.
AND WE HAVEN'T GOT ANY OF IT.
WHAT IDIOT SUGGESTED YOU PLAY IN GOAL, RACE?
WHAT... YOU DID...
GORDON STEWART'S ALIVE, OUR PHYSIO TELLS ME. GIVE HIM BACK HIS GOALIE'S SHIRT.
I'LL GIVE YOU THE LAST TEN MINUTES UP FRONT, RACE. SHOW US WHAT YOU CAN DO.
REALLY?
THANKS. I'LL NOT LET YOU DOWN, GAFFER!

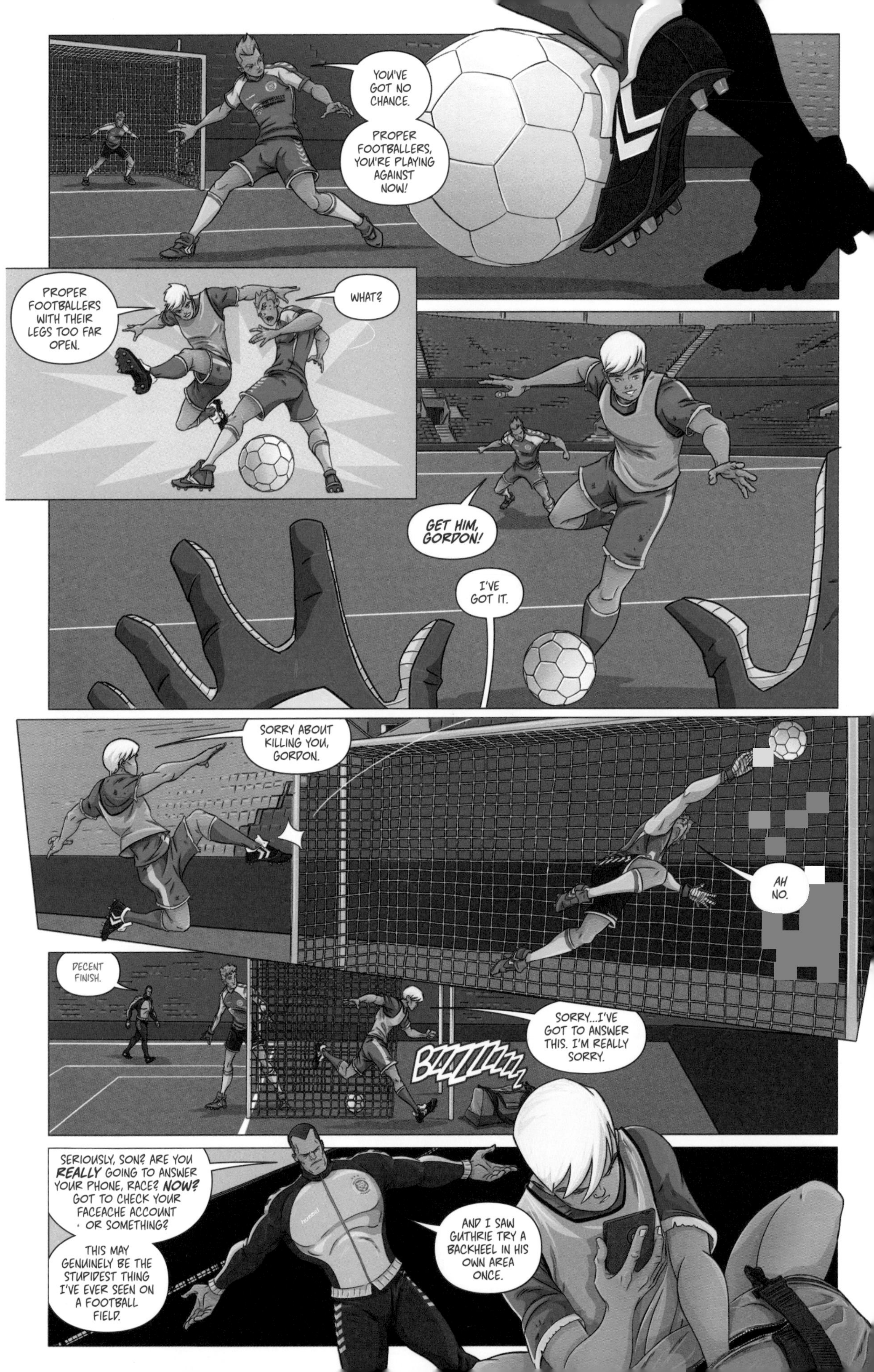

YOU'VE GOT NO CHANCE.
PROPER FOOTBALLERS, YOU'RE PLAYING AGAINST NOW!
PROPER FOOTBALLERS WITH THEIR LEGS TOO FAR OPEN.
WHAT?
GET HIM, GORDON!
I'VE GOT IT.
SORRY ABOUT KILLING YOU, GORDON.
AH NO.
DECENT FINISH.
SORRY...I'VE GOT TO ANSWER THIS. I'M REALLY SORRY.
BZZZZZZ
SERIOUSLY, SON? ARE YOU **REALLY** GOING TO ANSWER YOUR PHONE, RACE? **NOW?** GOT TO CHECK YOUR FACEACHE ACCOUNT OR SOMETHING?
THIS MAY GENUINELY BE THE STUPIDEST THING I'VE EVER SEEN ON A FOOTBALL FIELD.
AND I SAW GUTHRIE TRY A BACKHEEL IN HIS OWN AREA ONCE.

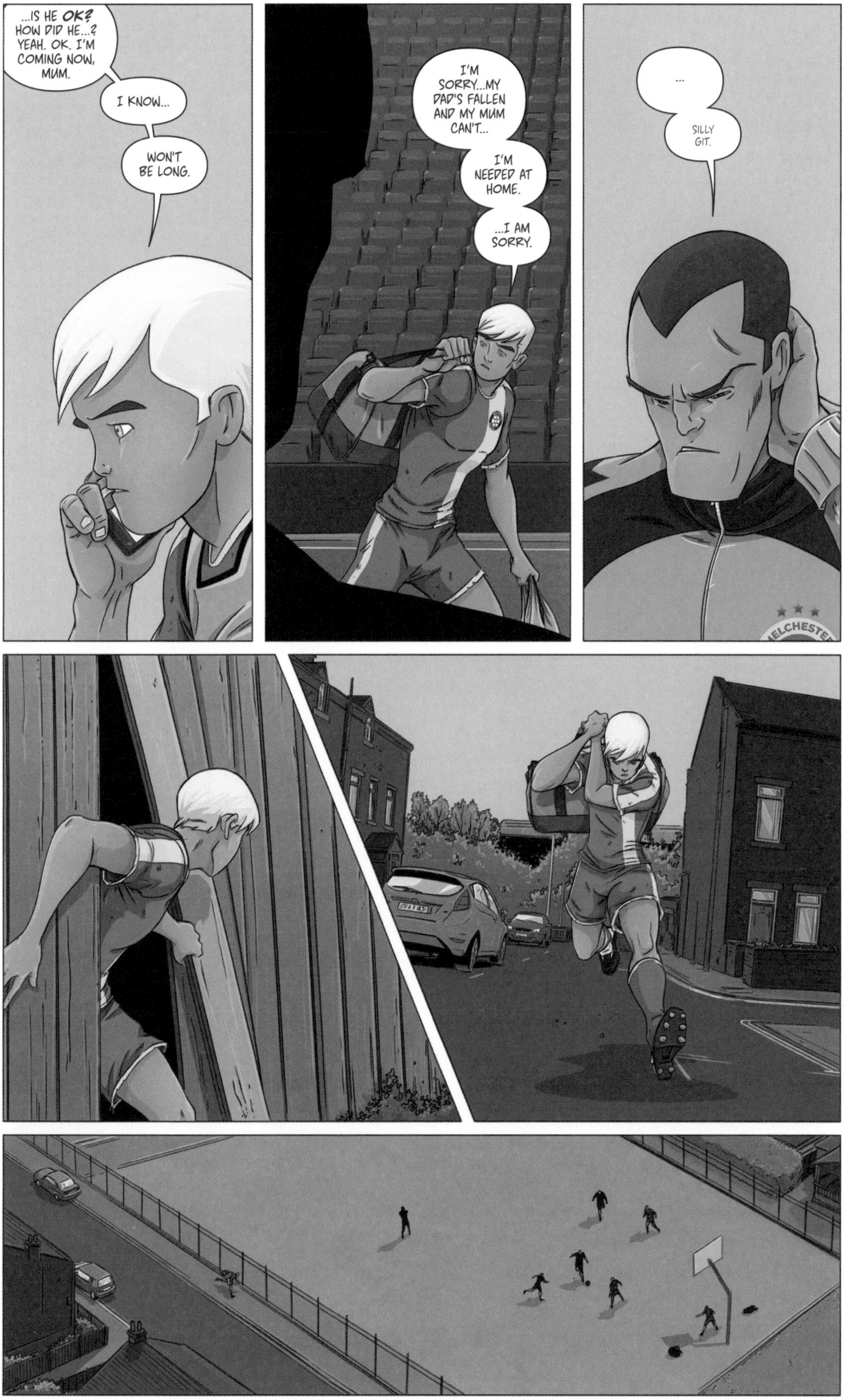
...IS HE OK? HOW DID HE...? YEAH. OK. I'M COMING NOW, MUM.
I KNOW...
WON'T BE LONG.
I'M SORRY...MY DAD'S FALLEN AND MY MUM CAN'T...
I'M NEEDED AT HOME.
...I AM SORRY.
...
SILLY GIT.

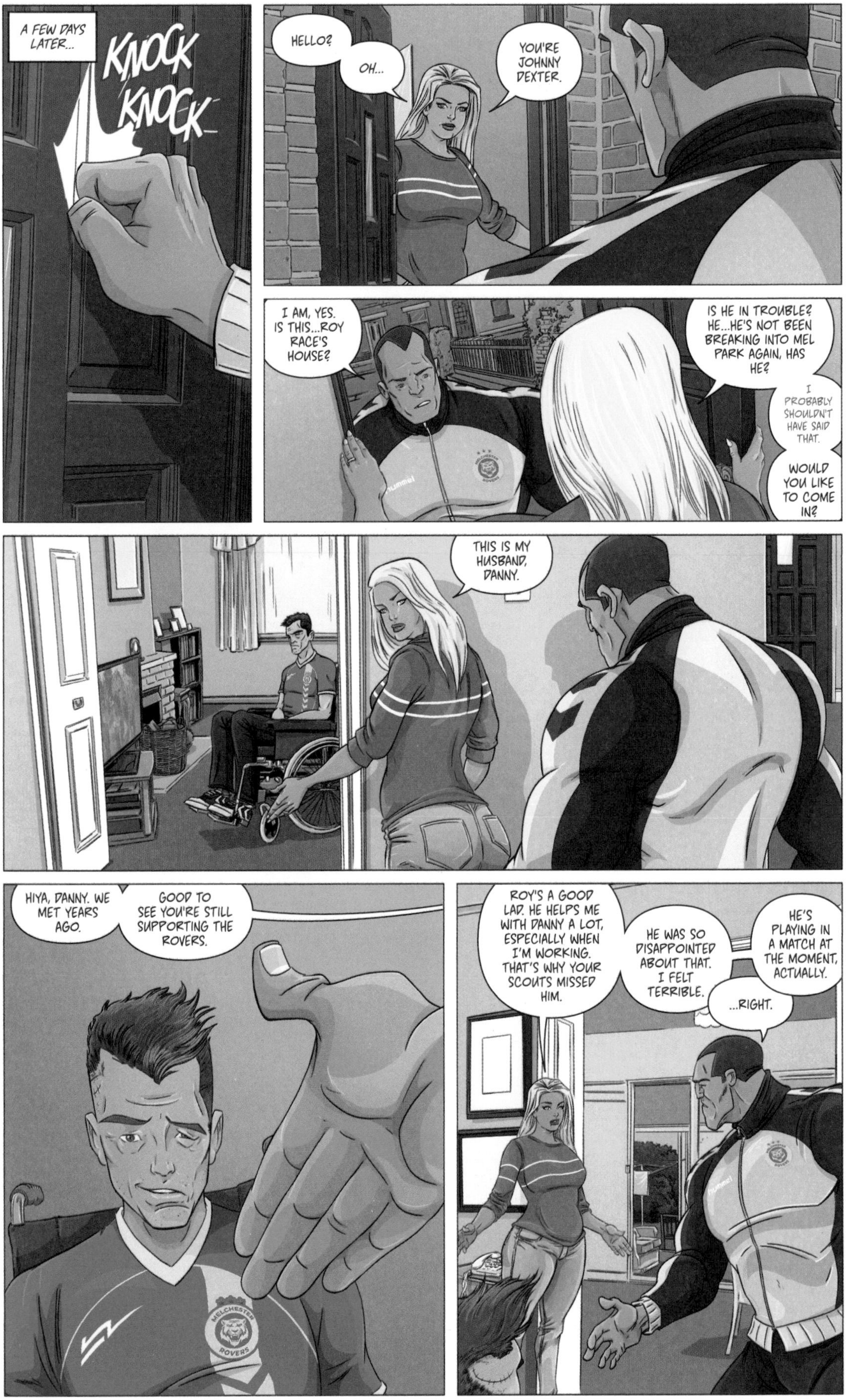
A FEW DAYS LATER...
KNOCK KNOCK
HELLO?
OH...
YOU'RE JOHNNY DEXTER.
I AM, YES. IS THIS...ROY RACE'S HOUSE?
IS HE IN TROUBLE? HE...HE'S NOT BEEN BREAKING INTO MEL PARK AGAIN, HAS HE?
I PROBABLY SHOULDN'T HAVE SAID THAT.
WOULD YOU LIKE TO COME IN?
THIS IS MY HUSBAND, DANNY.
HIYA, DANNY. WE MET YEARS AGO.
GOOD TO SEE YOU'RE STILL SUPPORTING THE ROVERS.
ROY'S A GOOD LAD. HE HELPS ME WITH DANNY A LOT, ESPECIALLY WHEN I'M WORKING. THAT'S WHY YOUR SCOUTS MISSED HIM.
HE WAS SO DISAPPOINTED ABOUT THAT. I FELT TERRIBLE.
HE'S PLAYING IN A MATCH AT THE MOMENT, ACTUALLY.
...RIGHT.

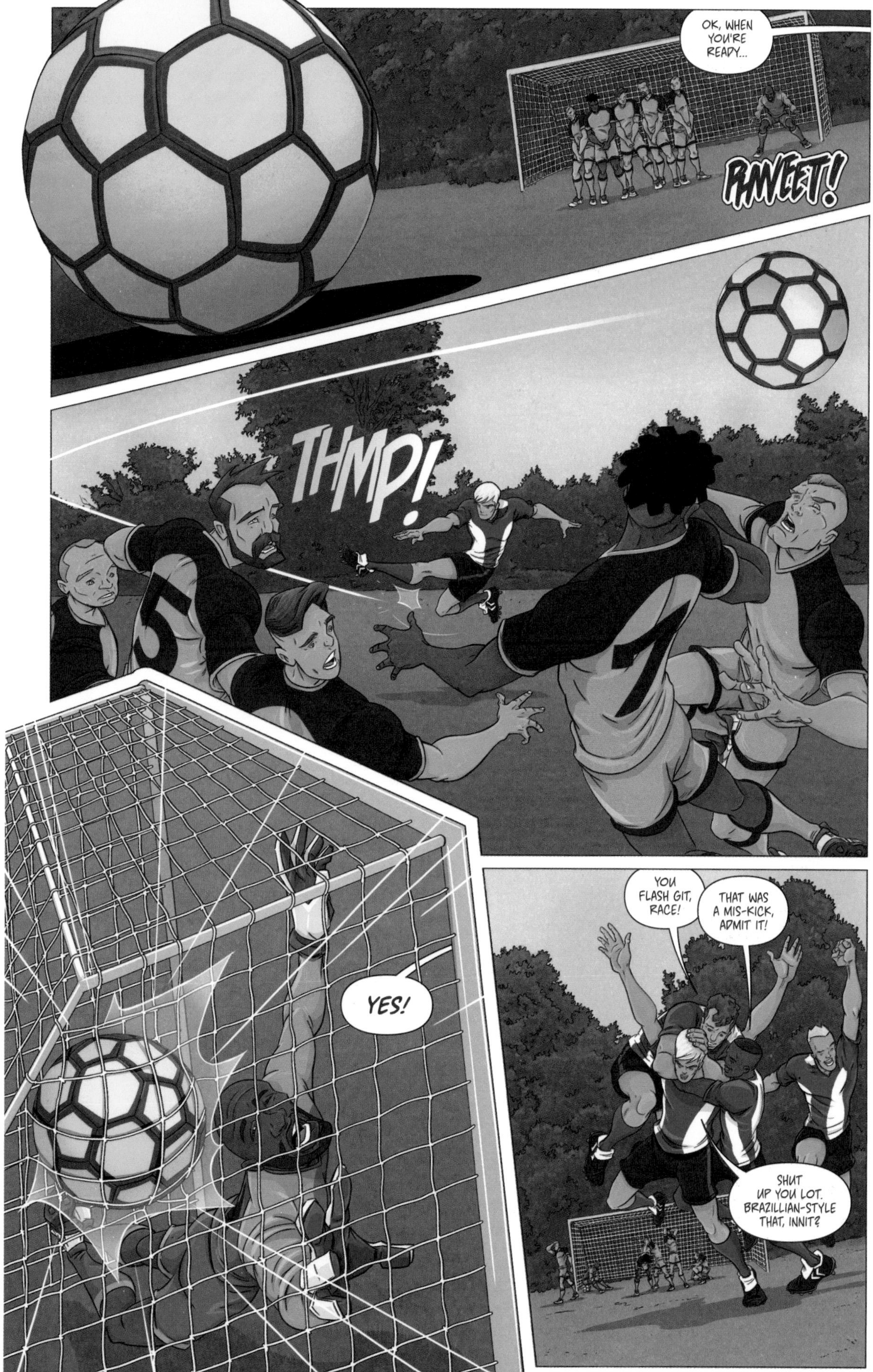
OK, WHEN YOU'RE READY...
PHWEET!
THMP!
YES!
YOU FLASH GIT, RACE!
THAT WAS A MIS-KICK, ADMIT IT!
SHUT UP YOU LOT. BRAZILLIAN-STYLE THAT, INNIT?

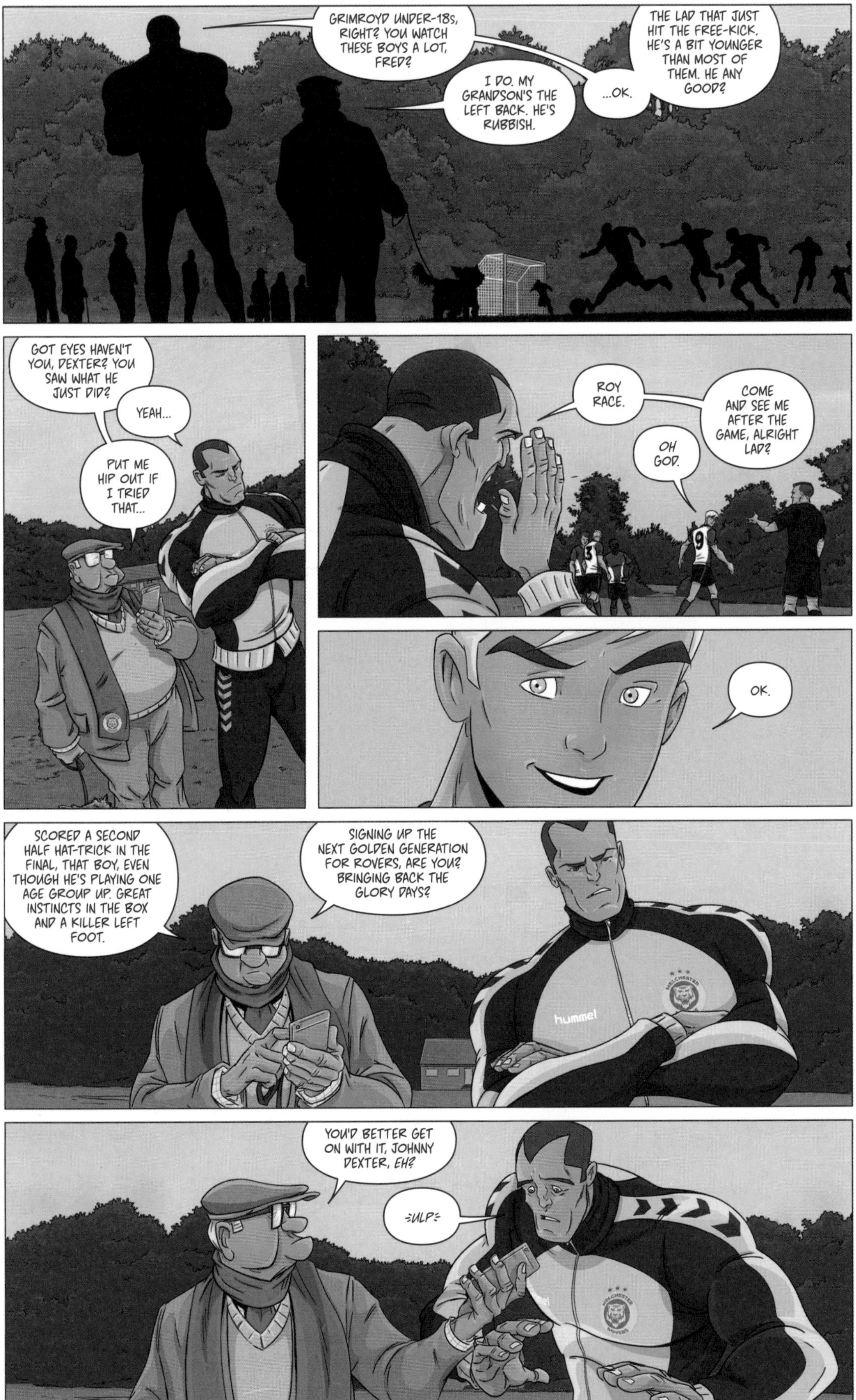
GRIMROYD UNDER-18s, RIGHT? YOU WATCH THESE BOYS A LOT, FRED?
I DO. MY GRANDSON'S THE LEFT BACK. HE'S RUBBISH.
...OK.
THE LAD THAT JUST HIT THE FREE-KICK. HE'S A BIT YOUNGER THAN MOST OF THEM. HE ANY GOOD?
GOT EYES HAVEN'T YOU, DEXTER? YOU SAW WHAT HE JUST DID?
YEAH...
PUT ME HIP OUT IF I TRIED THAT...
ROY RACE.
COME AND SEE ME AFTER THE GAME, ALRIGHT LAD?
OH GOD.
OK.
SCORED A SECOND HALF HAT-TRICK IN THE FINAL, THAT BOY, EVEN THOUGH HE'S PLAYING ONE AGE GROUP UP. GREAT INSTINCTS IN THE BOX AND A KILLER LEFT FOOT.
SIGNING UP THE NEXT GOLDEN GENERATION FOR ROVERS, ARE YOU? BRINGING BACK THE GLORY DAYS?
hummel
YOU'D BETTER GET ON WITH IT, JOHNNY DEXTER, EH?
ULP

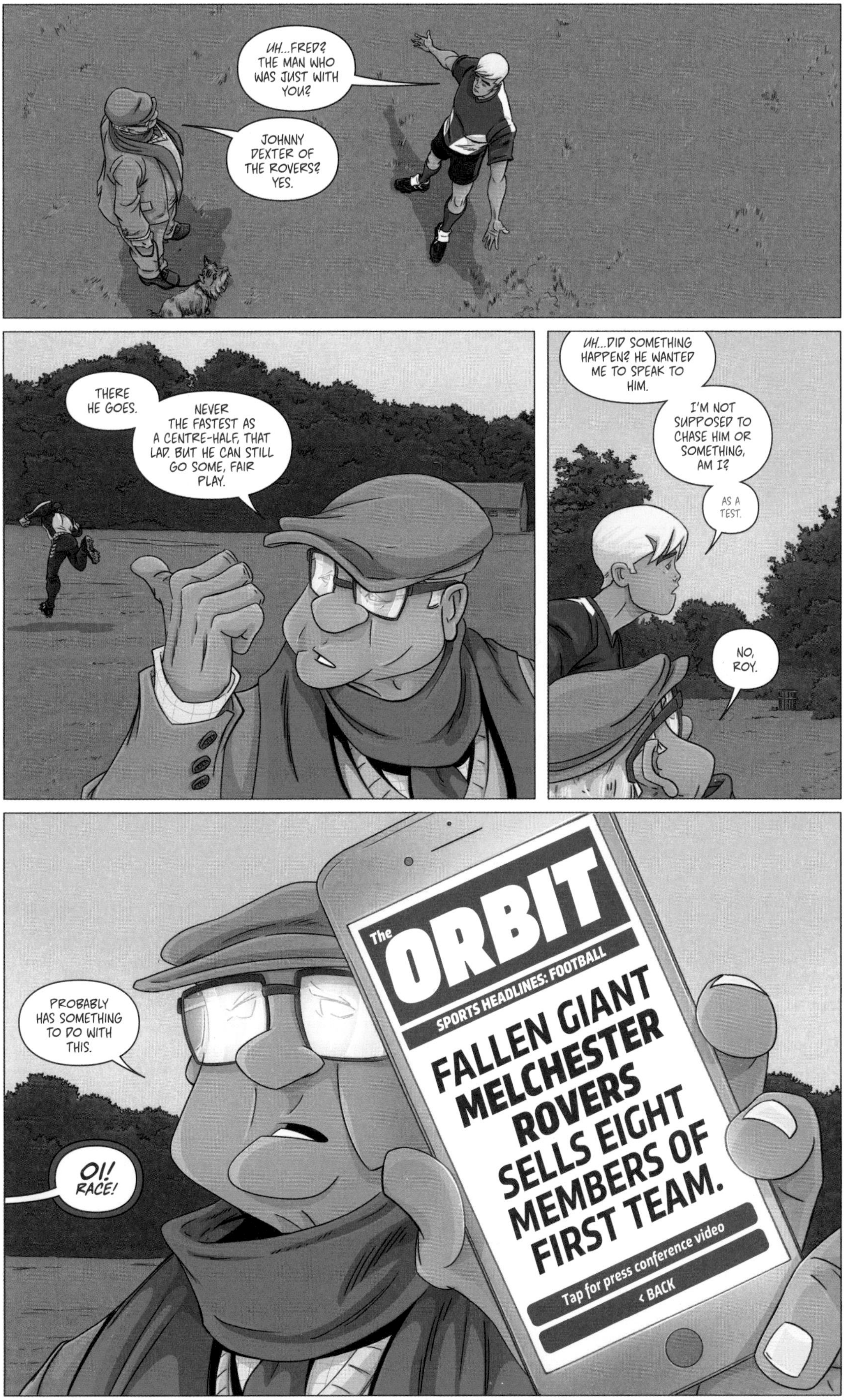
UH...FRED? THE MAN WHO WAS JUST WITH YOU?
JOHNNY DEXTER OF THE ROVERS? YES.
THERE HE GOES.
NEVER THE FASTEST AS A CENTRE-HALF, THAT LAD. BUT HE CAN STILL GO SOME, FAIR PLAY.
UH...DID SOMETHING HAPPEN? HE WANTED ME TO SPEAK TO HIM.
I'M NOT SUPPOSED TO CHASE HIM OR SOMETHING, AM I?
AS A TEST.
NO, ROY.
PROBABLY HAS SOMETHING TO DO WITH THIS.
The ORBIT
SPORTS HEADLINES: FOOTBALL
FALLEN GIANT MELCHESTER ROVERS SELLS EIGHT MEMBERS OF FIRST TEAM.
Tap for press conference video
< BACK
OI! RACE!

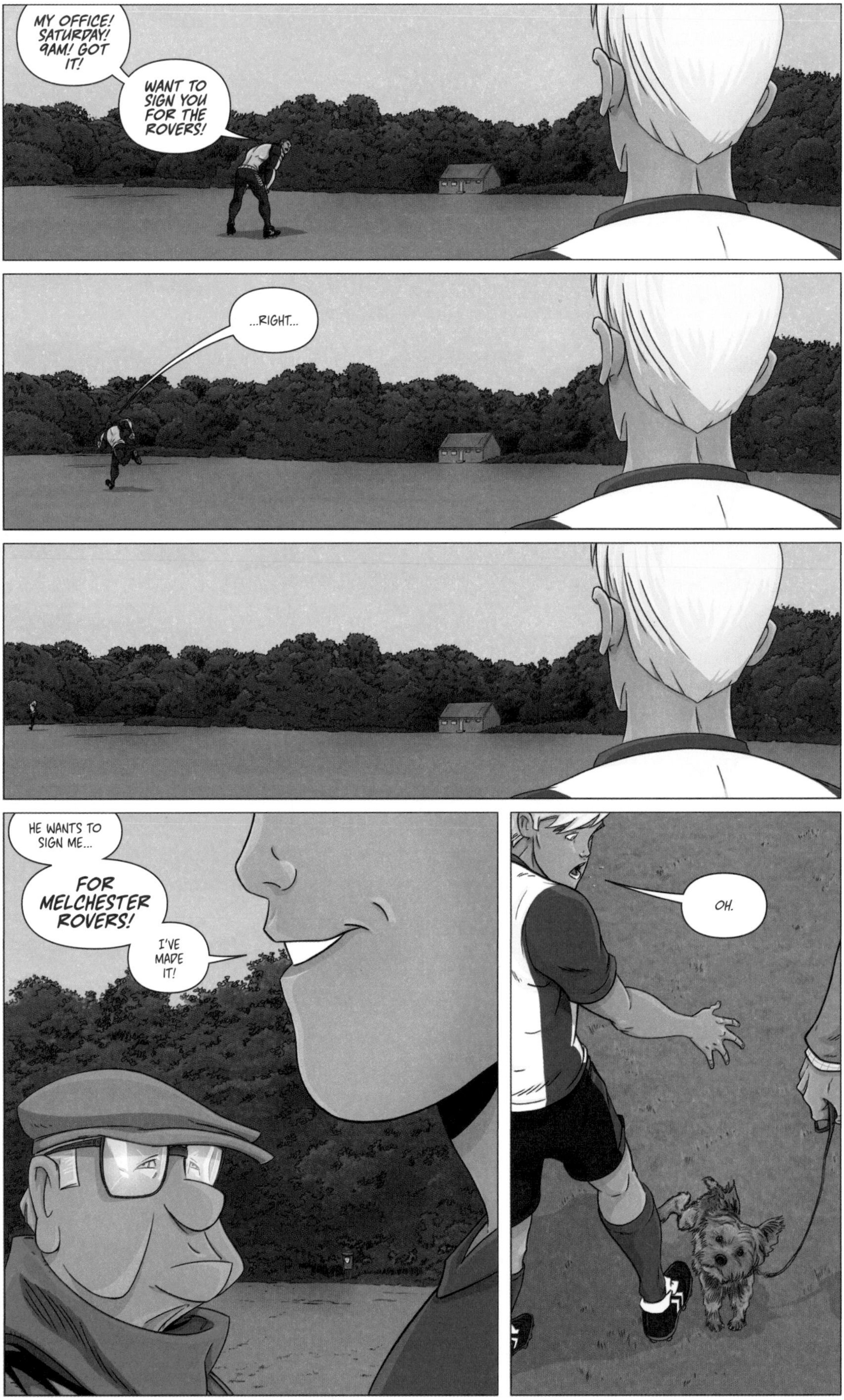
MY OFFICE! SATURDAY! 9AM! GOT IT!
WANT TO SIGN YOU FOR THE ROVERS!
...RIGHT...
HE WANTS TO SIGN ME...
FOR MELCHESTER ROVERS!
I'VE MADE IT!
OH.

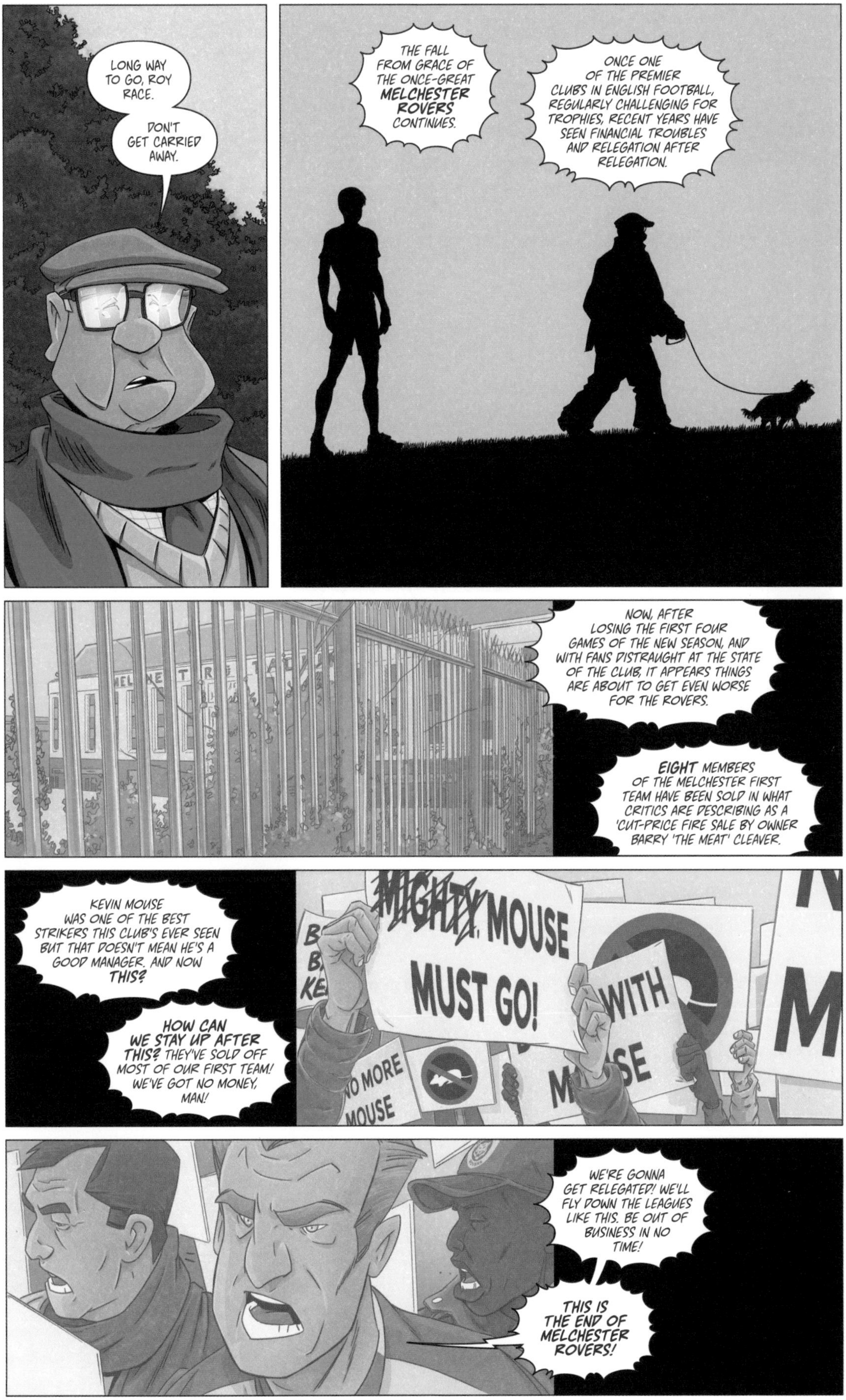
LONG WAY TO GO, ROY RACE.
DON'T GET CARRIED AWAY.
THE FALL FROM GRACE OF THE ONCE-GREAT **MELCHESTER ROVERS** CONTINUES.
ONCE ONE OF THE PREMIER CLUBS IN ENGLISH FOOTBALL, REGULARLY CHALLENGING FOR TROPHIES, RECENT YEARS HAVE SEEN FINANCIAL TROUBLES AND RELEGATION AFTER RELEGATION.
NOW, AFTER LOSING THE FIRST FOUR GAMES OF THE NEW SEASON, AND WITH FANS DISTRAUGHT AT THE STATE OF THE CLUB, IT APPEARS THINGS ARE ABOUT TO GET EVEN WORSE FOR THE ROVERS.
EIGHT MEMBERS OF THE MELCHESTER FIRST TEAM HAVE BEEN SOLD IN WHAT CRITICS ARE DESCRIBING AS A 'CUT-PRICE FIRE SALE BY OWNER BARRY 'THE MEAT' CLEAVER.
KEVIN MOUSE WAS ONE OF THE BEST STRIKERS THIS CLUB'S EVER SEEN BUT THAT DOESN'T MEAN HE'S A GOOD MANAGER. AND NOW **THIS?**
HOW CAN WE STAY UP AFTER THIS? THEY'VE SOLD OFF MOST OF OUR FIRST TEAM! WE'VE GOT NO MONEY, MAN!
~~MIGHTY~~ MOUSE MUST GO!
WITH
NO MORE MOUSE
WE'RE GONNA GET RELEGATED! WE'LL FLY DOWN THE LEAGUES LIKE THIS. BE OUT OF BUSINESS IN NO TIME!
THIS IS THE END OF MELCHESTER ROVERS!

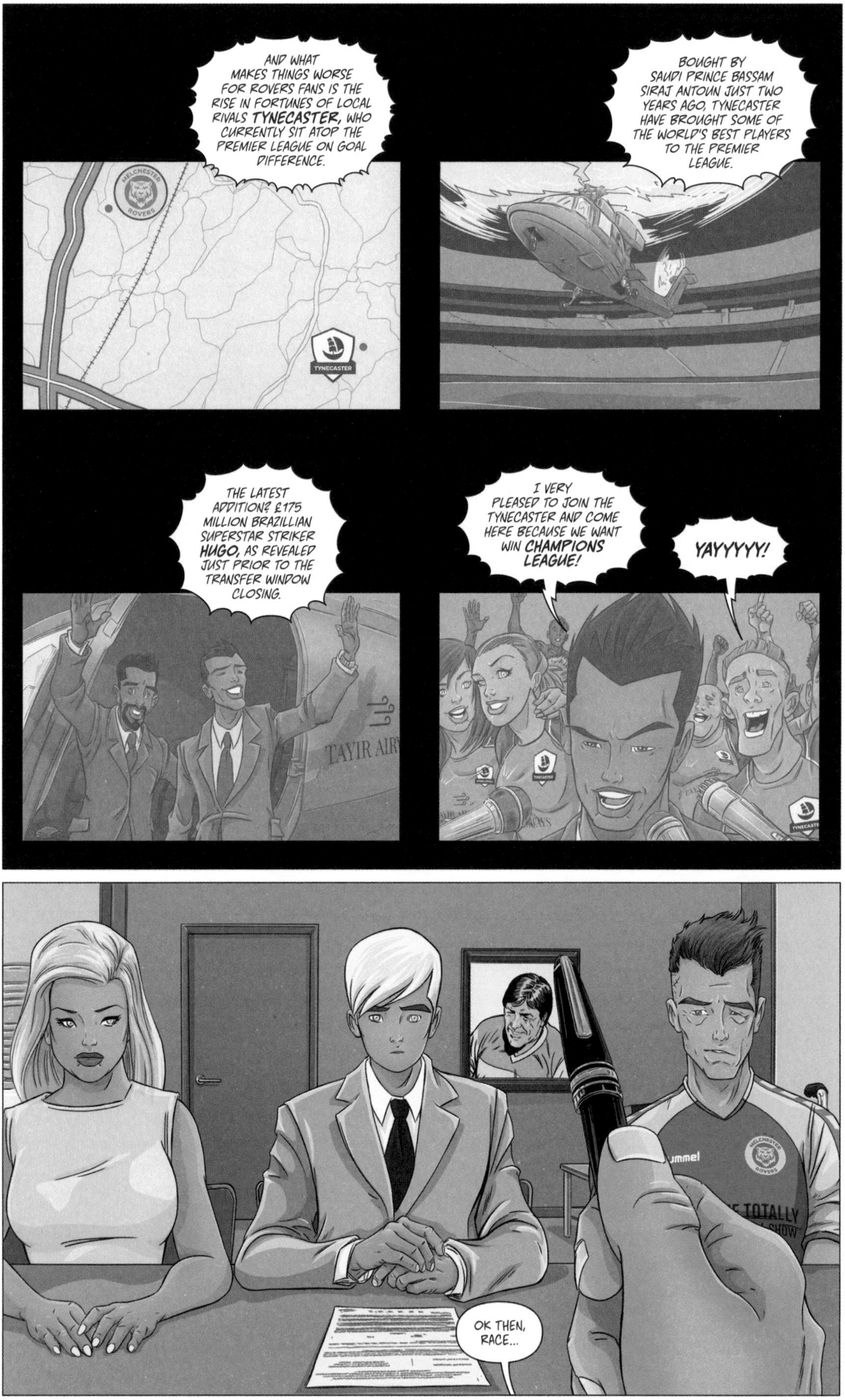
AND WHAT MAKES THINGS WORSE FOR ROVERS FANS IS THE RISE IN FORTUNES OF LOCAL RIVALS **TYNECASTER,** WHO CURRENTLY SIT ATOP THE PREMIER LEAGUE ON GOAL DIFFERENCE.
MELCHESTER ROVERS
TYNECASTER
BOUGHT BY SAUDI PRINCE BASSAM SIRAJ ANTOUN JUST TWO YEARS AGO, TYNECASTER HAVE BROUGHT SOME OF THE WORLD'S BEST PLAYERS TO THE PREMIER LEAGUE.
THE LATEST ADDITION? £175 MILLION BRAZILLIAN SUPERSTAR STRIKER **HUGO,** AS REVEALED JUST PRIOR TO THE TRANSFER WINDOW CLOSING.
I VERY PLEASED TO JOIN THE TYNECASTER AND COME HERE BECAUSE WE WANT WIN **CHAMPIONS LEAGUE!**
YAYYYYY!
OK THEN, RACE...

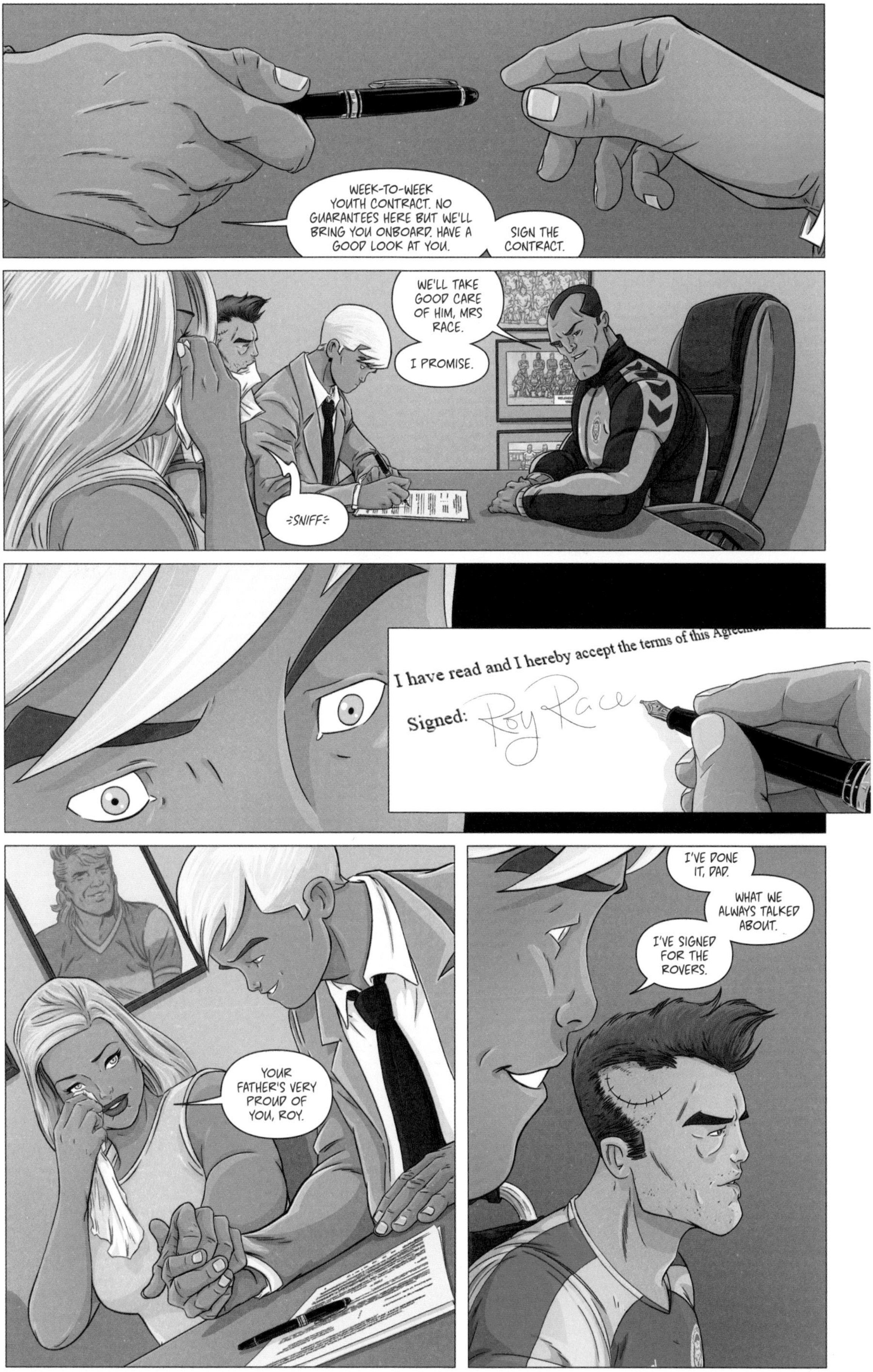
WEEK-TO-WEEK YOUTH CONTRACT. NO GUARANTEES HERE BUT WE'LL BRING YOU ONBOARD. HAVE A GOOD LOOK AT YOU.
SIGN THE CONTRACT.
WE'LL TAKE GOOD CARE OF HIM, MRS RACE.
I PROMISE.
=SNIFF=
I have read and I hereby accept the terms of this Agreement
Signed: Roy Race
YOUR FATHER'S VERY PROUD OF YOU, ROY.
I'VE DONE IT, DAD.
WHAT WE ALWAYS TALKED ABOUT.
I'VE SIGNED FOR THE ROVERS.

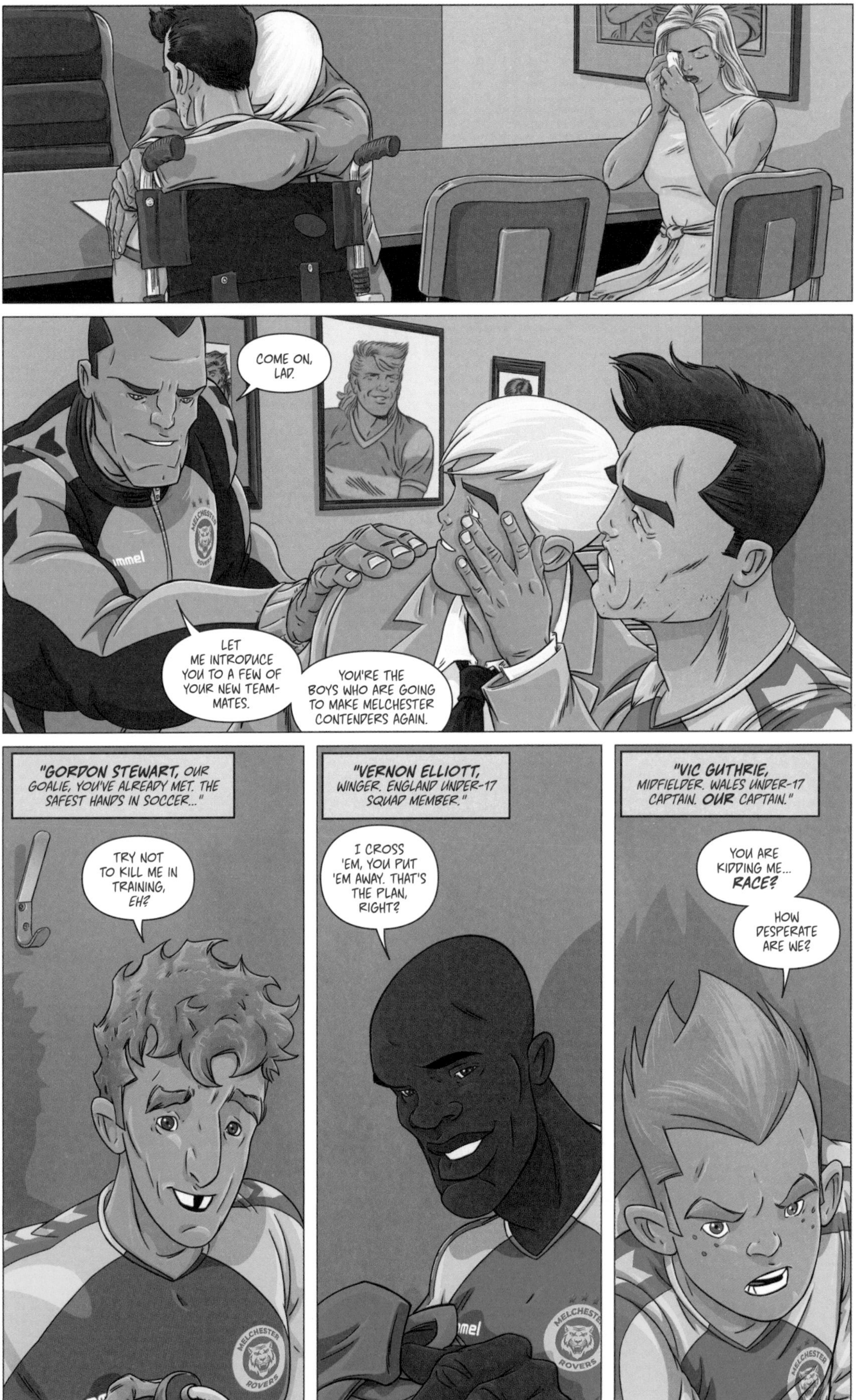
COME ON, LAD.
LET ME INTRODUCE YOU TO A FEW OF YOUR NEW TEAM-MATES.
YOU'RE THE BOYS WHO ARE GOING TO MAKE MELCHESTER CONTENDERS AGAIN.
"GORDON STEWART, OUR GOALIE, YOU'VE ALREADY MET. THE SAFEST HANDS IN SOCCER..."
TRY NOT TO KILL ME IN TRAINING, EH?
"VERNON ELLIOTT, WINGER. ENGLAND UNDER-17 SQUAD MEMBER."
I CROSS 'EM, YOU PUT 'EM AWAY. THAT'S THE PLAN, RIGHT?
"VIC GUTHRIE, MIDFIELDER. WALES UNDER-17 CAPTAIN. OUR CAPTAIN."
YOU ARE KIDDING ME... RACE?
HOW DESPERATE ARE WE?

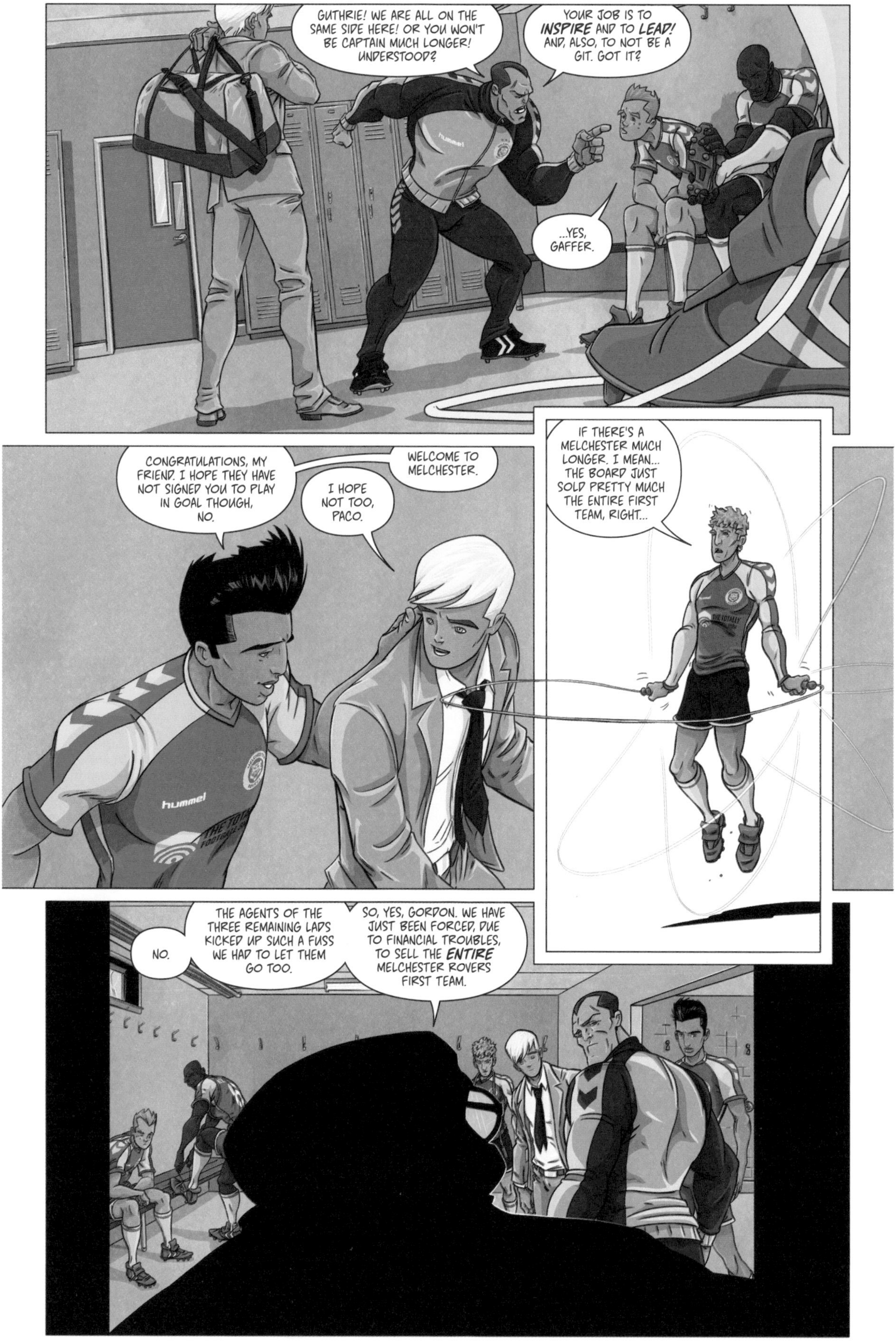
GUTHRIE! WE ARE ALL ON THE SAME SIDE HERE! OR YOU WON'T BE CAPTAIN MUCH LONGER! UNDERSTOOD?
YOUR JOB IS TO ***INSPIRE*** AND TO ***LEAD!*** AND, ALSO, TO NOT BE A GIT. GOT IT?
...YES, GAFFER.
hummel
CONGRATULATIONS, MY FRIEND. I HOPE THEY HAVE NOT SIGNED YOU TO PLAY IN GOAL THOUGH, NO.
WELCOME TO MELCHESTER.
I HOPE NOT TOO, PACO.
hummel
IF THERE'S A MELCHESTER MUCH LONGER. I MEAN... THE BOARD JUST SOLD PRETTY MUCH THE ENTIRE FIRST TEAM, RIGHT...
SO, YES, GORDON. WE HAVE JUST BEEN FORCED, DUE TO FINANCIAL TROUBLES, TO SELL THE ***ENTIRE*** MELCHESTER ROVERS FIRST TEAM.
NO.
THE AGENTS OF THE THREE REMAINING LADS KICKED UP SUCH A FUSS WE HAD TO LET THEM GO TOO.

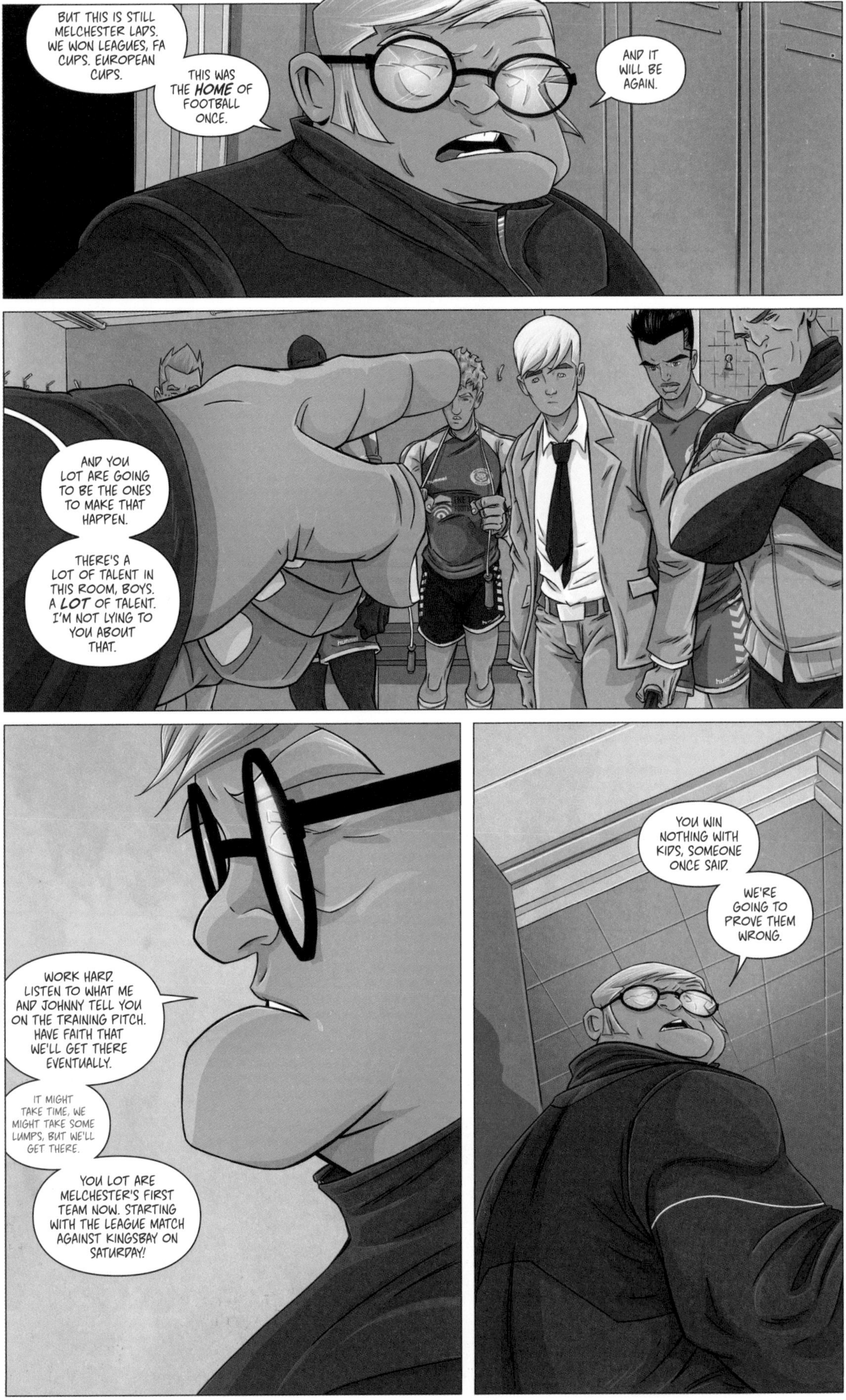
BUT THIS IS STILL MELCHESTER LADS. WE WON LEAGUES, FA CUPS. EUROPEAN CUPS.
THIS WAS THE HOME OF FOOTBALL ONCE.
AND IT WILL BE AGAIN.
AND YOU LOT ARE GOING TO BE THE ONES TO MAKE THAT HAPPEN.
THERE'S A LOT OF TALENT IN THIS ROOM, BOYS. A LOT OF TALENT. I'M NOT LYING TO YOU ABOUT THAT.
WORK HARD. LISTEN TO WHAT ME AND JOHNNY TELL YOU ON THE TRAINING PITCH. HAVE FAITH THAT WE'LL GET THERE EVENTUALLY.
IT MIGHT TAKE TIME, WE MIGHT TAKE SOME LUMPS, BUT WE'LL GET THERE.
YOU LOT ARE MELCHESTER'S FIRST TEAM NOW. STARTING WITH THE LEAGUE MATCH AGAINST KINGSBAY ON SATURDAY!
YOU WIN NOTHING WITH KIDS, SOMEONE ONCE SAID.
WE'RE GOING TO PROVE THEM WRONG.

WHAT JUST HAPPENED?

A GOOD DAY TO JOIN THE CLUB, EH?

ROY OF THE ROVERS.

HALF TIME!

GO HAVE AN ORANGE SLICE AND A DRINK OF WATER!

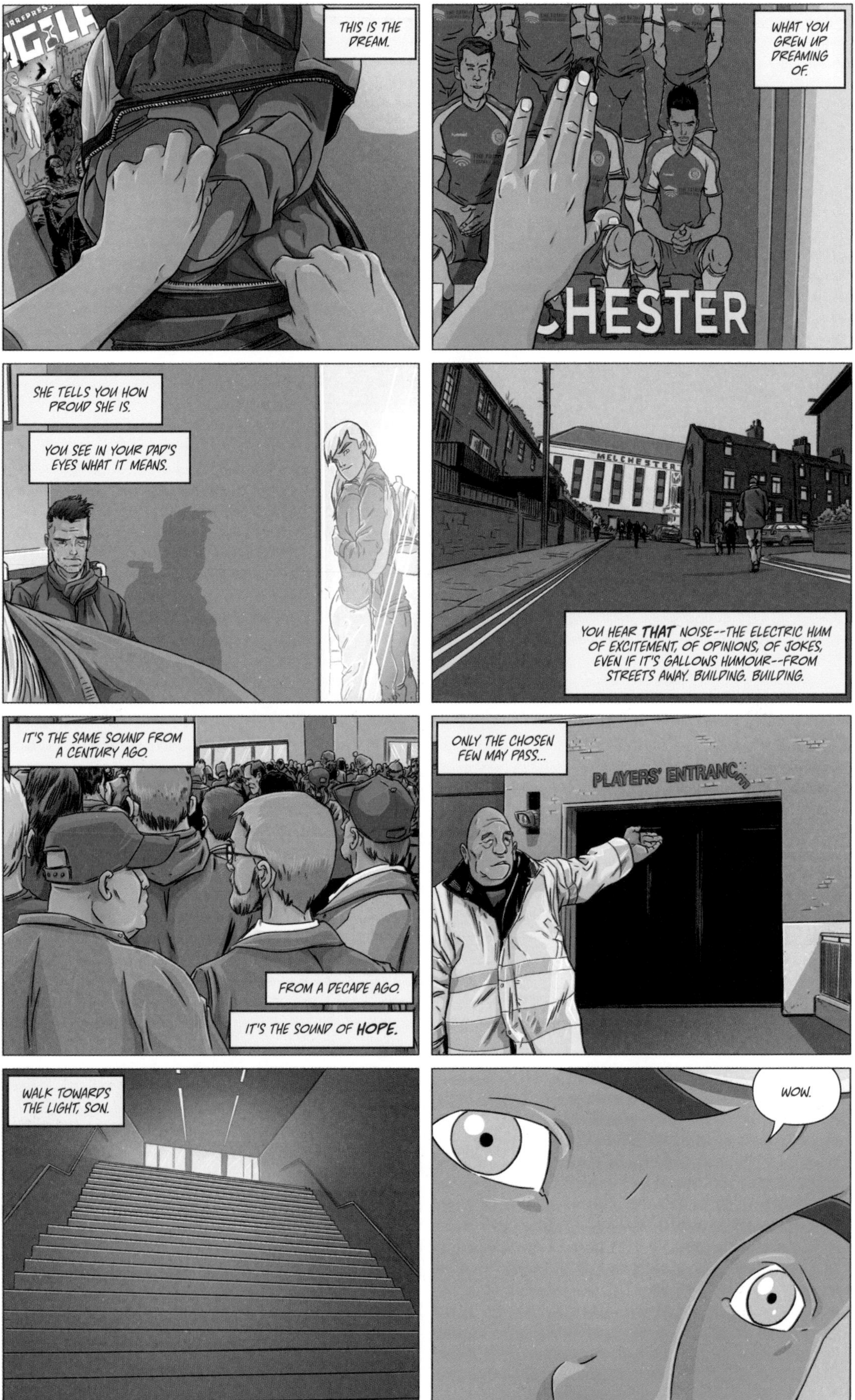
THIS IS THE DREAM.
WHAT YOU GREW UP DREAMING OF.
CHESTER
SHE TELLS YOU HOW PROUD SHE IS.
YOU SEE IN YOUR DAD'S EYES WHAT IT MEANS.
MELCHESTER
YOU HEAR THAT NOISE--THE ELECTRIC HUM OF EXCITEMENT, OF OPINIONS, OF JOKES, EVEN IF IT'S GALLOWS HUMOUR--FROM STREETS AWAY. BUILDING. BUILDING.
IT'S THE SAME SOUND FROM A CENTURY AGO.
FROM A DECADE AGO.
IT'S THE SOUND OF HOPE.
ONLY THE CHOSEN FEW MAY PASS...
PLAYERS' ENTRANC
WALK TOWARDS THE LIGHT, SON.
WOW.

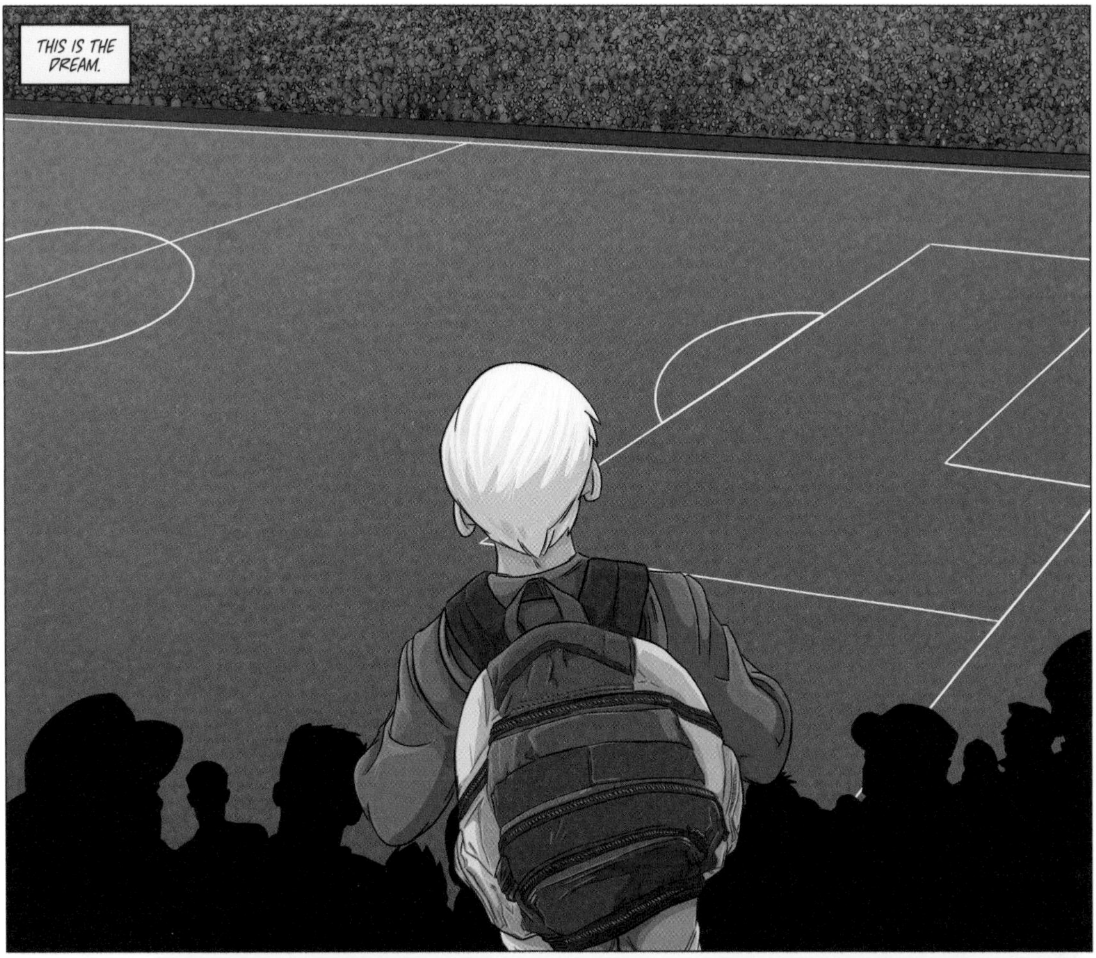
THIS IS THE DREAM.

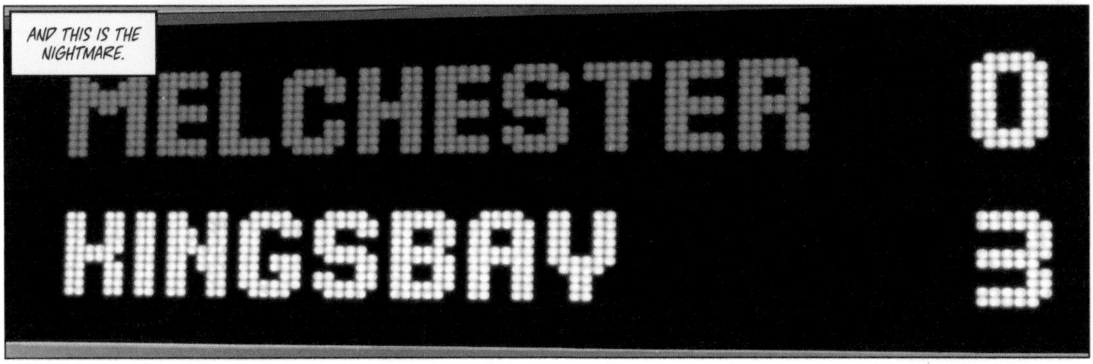
AND THIS IS THE NIGHTMARE.
MELCHESTER 0
KINGSBAY 3

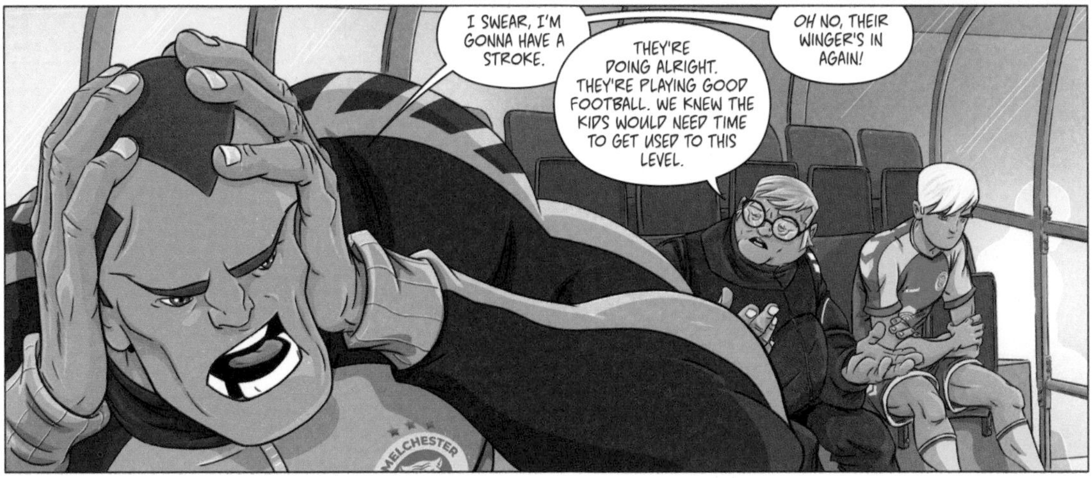
I SWEAR, I'M GONNA HAVE A STROKE.
THEY'RE DOING ALRIGHT. THEY'RE PLAYING GOOD FOOTBALL. WE KNEW THE KIDS WOULD NEED TIME TO GET USED TO THIS LEVEL.
OH NO, THEIR WINGER'S IN AGAIN!
MELCHESTER

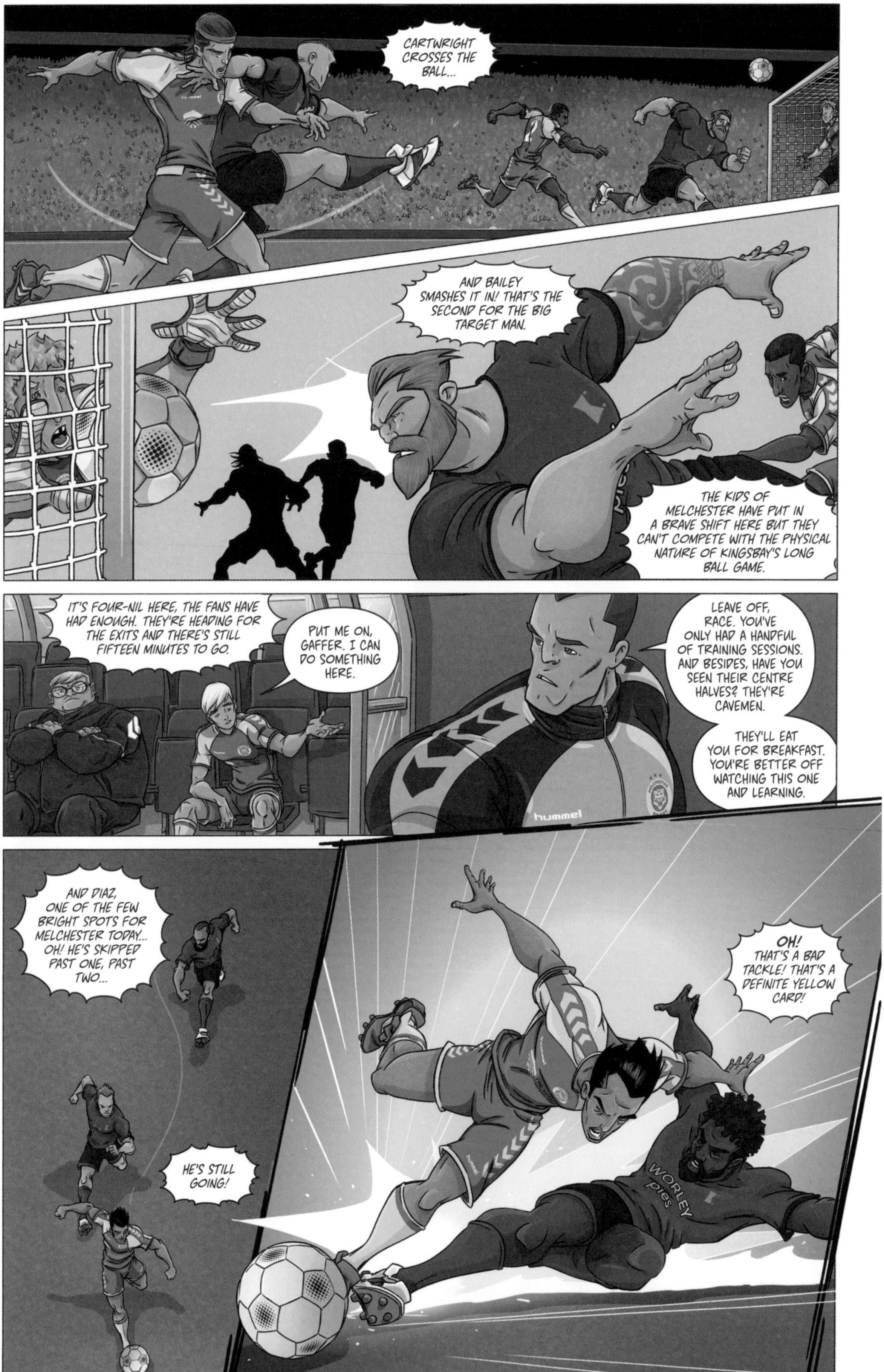
CARTWRIGHT CROSSES THE BALL...
AND BAILEY SMASHES IT IN! THAT'S THE SECOND FOR THE BIG TARGET MAN.
THE KIDS OF MELCHESTER HAVE PUT IN A BRAVE SHIFT HERE BUT THEY CAN'T COMPETE WITH THE PHYSICAL NATURE OF KINGSBAY'S LONG BALL GAME.
IT'S FOUR-NIL HERE, THE FANS HAVE HAD ENOUGH. THEY'RE HEADING FOR THE EXITS AND THERE'S STILL FIFTEEN MINUTES TO GO.
PUT ME ON, GAFFER. I CAN DO SOMETHING HERE.
LEAVE OFF, RACE. YOU'VE ONLY HAD A HANDFUL OF TRAINING SESSIONS. AND BESIDES, HAVE YOU SEEN THEIR CENTRE HALVES? THEY'RE CAVEMEN.
THEY'LL EAT YOU FOR BREAKFAST. YOU'RE BETTER OFF WATCHING THIS ONE AND LEARNING.
hummel
AND DIAZ, ONE OF THE FEW BRIGHT SPOTS FOR MELCHESTER TODAY... OH! HE'S SKIPPED PAST ONE, PAST TWO...
HE'S STILL GOING!
OH! THAT'S A BAD TACKLE! THAT'S A DEFINITE YELLOW CARD!
WORLEY pies

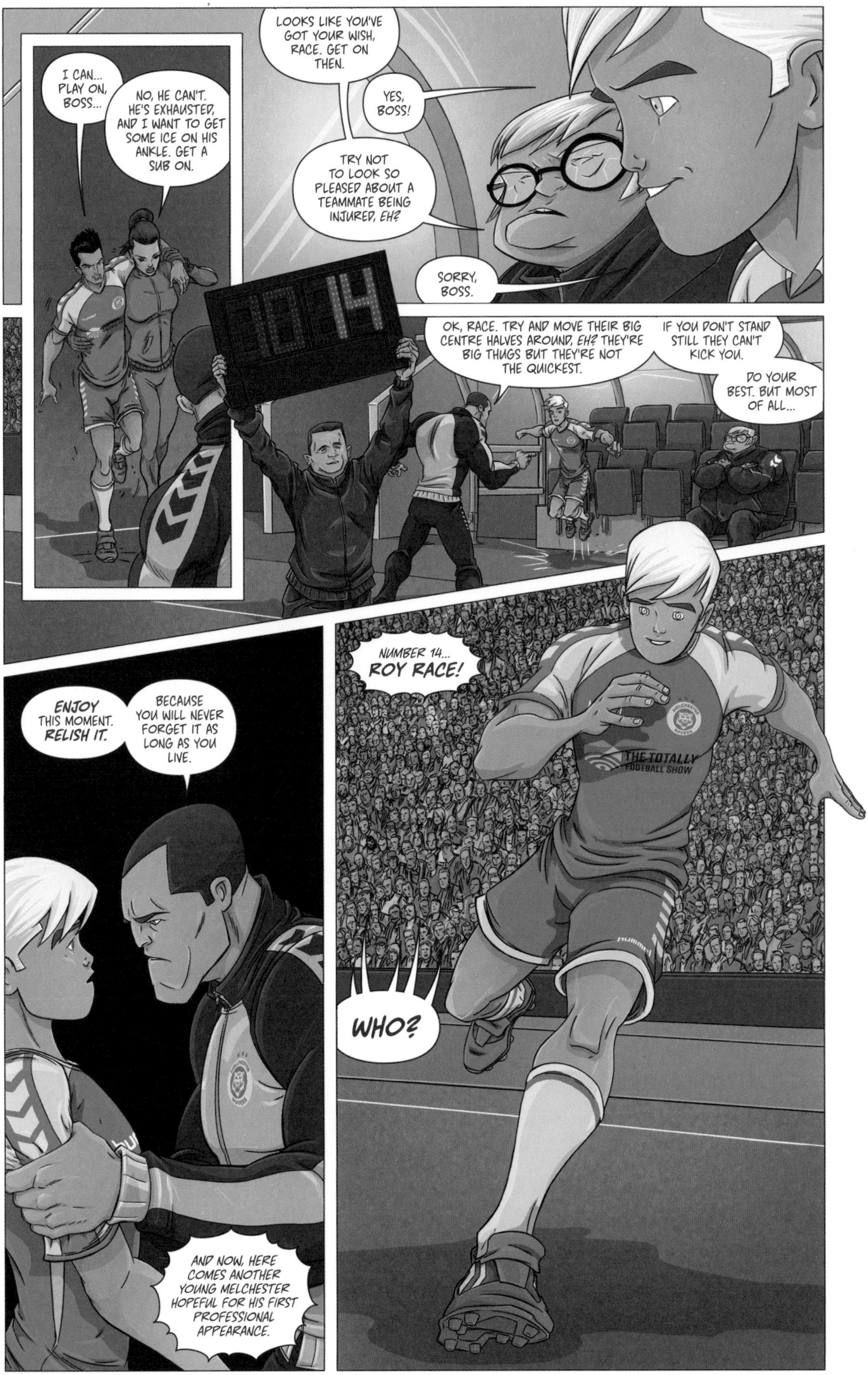
I CAN... PLAY ON, BOSS...
NO, HE CAN'T. HE'S EXHAUSTED, AND I WANT TO GET SOME ICE ON HIS ANKLE. GET A SUB ON.
LOOKS LIKE YOU'VE GOT YOUR WISH, RACE. GET ON THEN.
YES, BOSS!
TRY NOT TO LOOK SO PLEASED ABOUT A TEAMMATE BEING INJURED, EH?
SORRY, BOSS.
10 14
OK, RACE. TRY AND MOVE THEIR BIG CENTRE HALVES AROUND, EH? THEY'RE BIG THUGS BUT THEY'RE NOT THE QUICKEST.
IF YOU DON'T STAND STILL THEY CAN'T KICK YOU.
DO YOUR BEST. BUT MOST OF ALL...
ENJOY THIS MOMENT. RELISH IT.
BECAUSE YOU WILL NEVER FORGET IT AS LONG AS YOU LIVE.
AND NOW, HERE COMES ANOTHER YOUNG MELCHESTER HOPEFUL FOR HIS FIRST PROFESSIONAL APPEARANCE.
NUMBER 14... ROY RACE!
WHO?
THE TOTALLY FOOTBALL SHOW

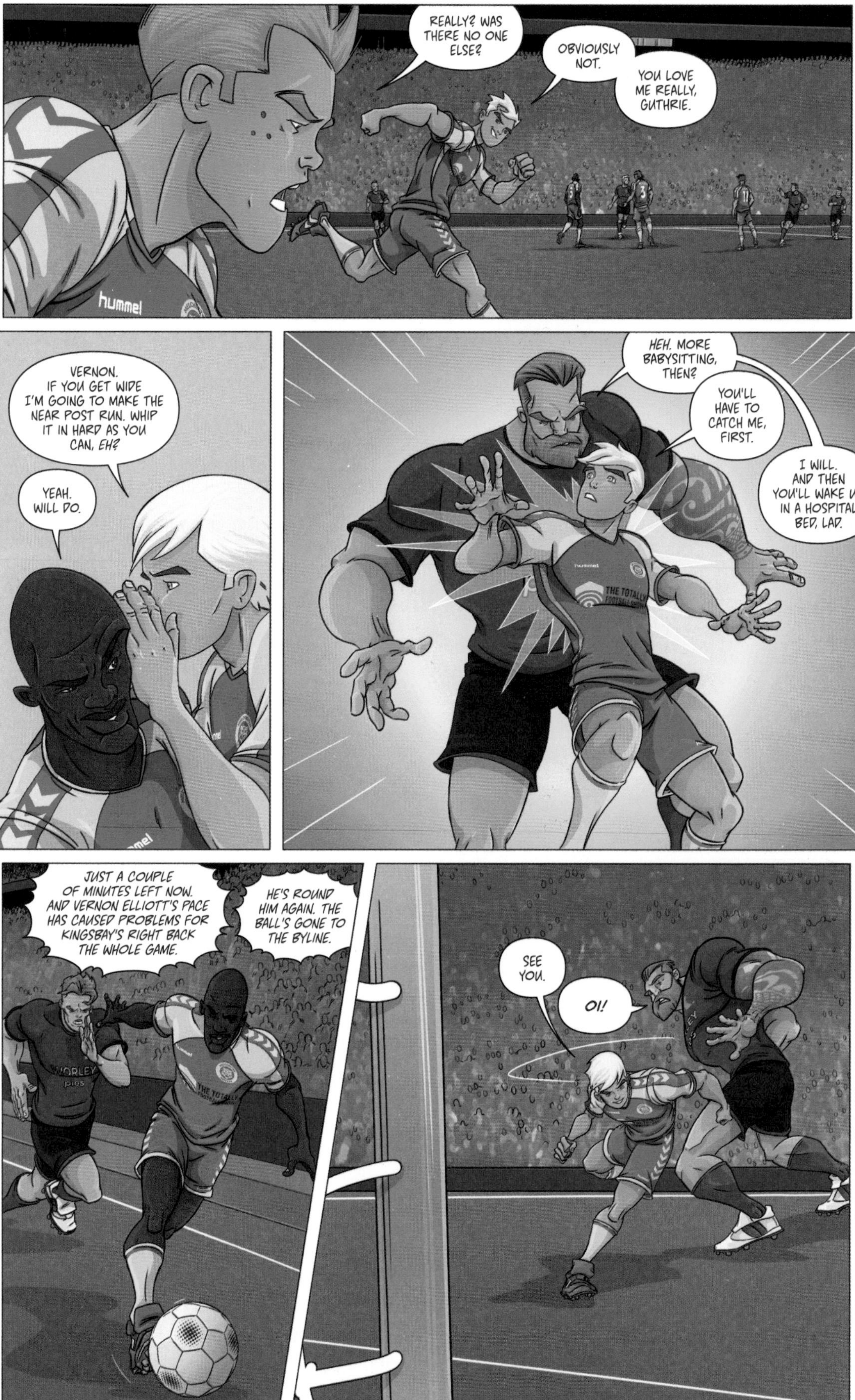
REALLY? WAS THERE NO ONE ELSE?
OBVIOUSLY NOT.
YOU LOVE ME REALLY, GUTHRIE.
hummel
VERNON. IF YOU GET WIDE I'M GOING TO MAKE THE NEAR POST RUN. WHIP IT IN HARD AS YOU CAN, EH?
YEAH. WILL DO.
HEH. MORE BABYSITTING, THEN?
YOU'LL HAVE TO CATCH ME, FIRST.
I WILL. AND THEN YOU'LL WAKE UP IN A HOSPITAL BED, LAD.
JUST A COUPLE OF MINUTES LEFT NOW. AND VERNON ELLIOTT'S PACE HAS CAUSED PROBLEMS FOR KINGSBAY'S RIGHT BACK THE WHOLE GAME.
HE'S ROUND HIM AGAIN. THE BALL'S GONE TO THE BYLINE.
SEE YOU.
OI!

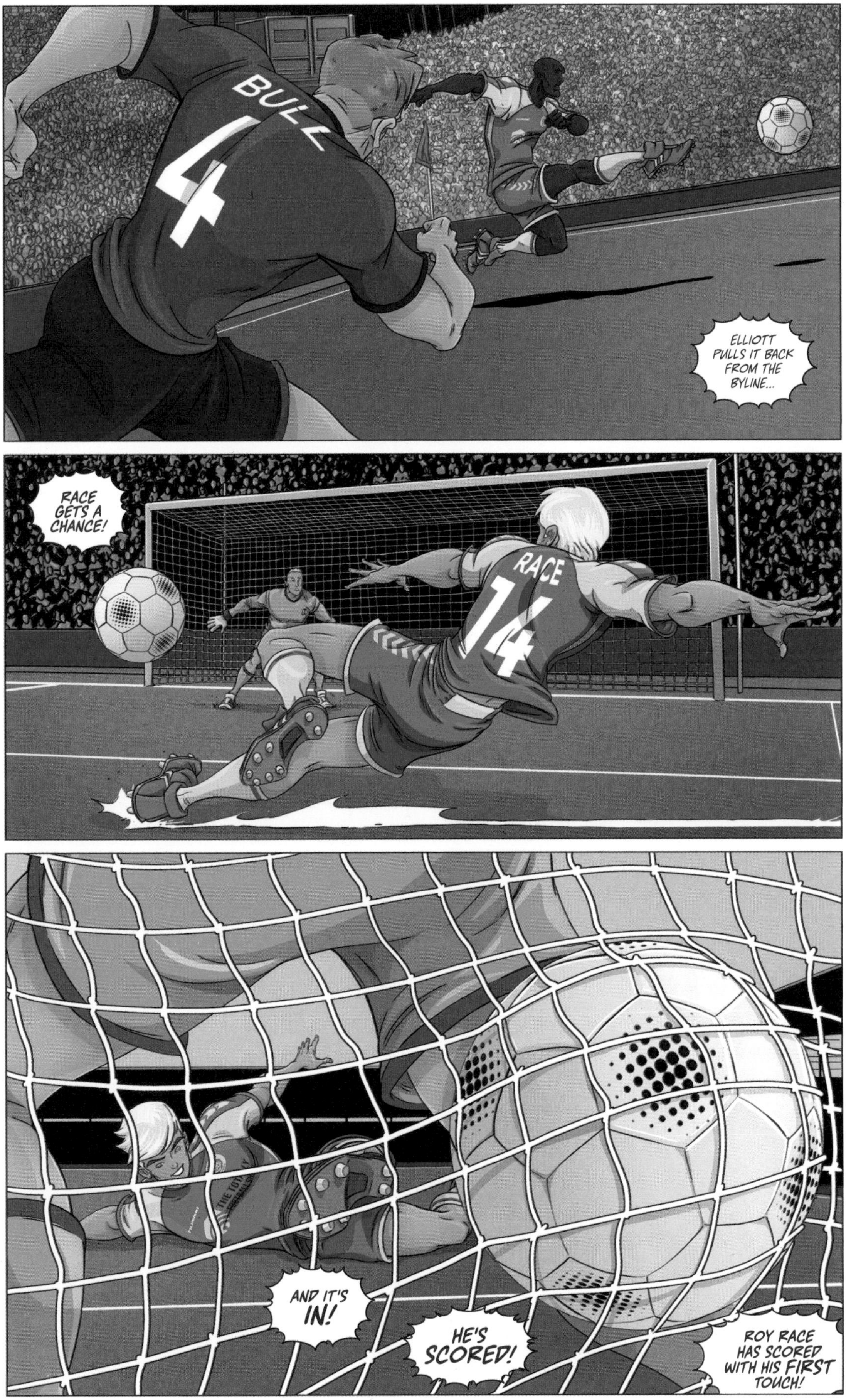
ELLIOTT PULLS IT BACK FROM THE BYLINE...
RACE GETS A CHANCE!
AND IT'S IN!
HE'S SCORED!
ROY RACE HAS SCORED WITH HIS FIRST TOUCH!

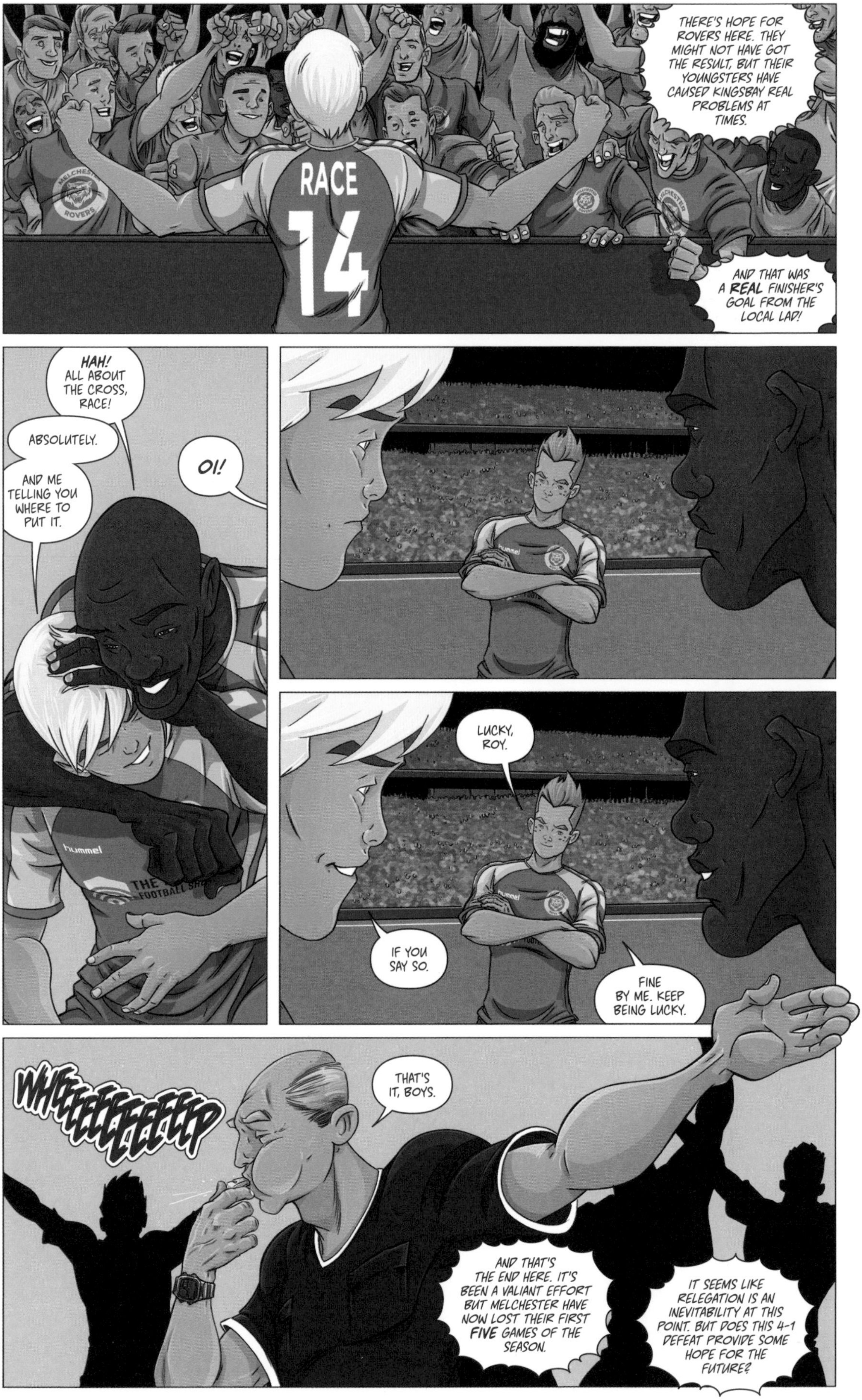
THERE'S HOPE FOR ROVERS HERE. THEY MIGHT NOT HAVE GOT THE RESULT, BUT THEIR YOUNGSTERS HAVE CAUSED KINGSBAY REAL PROBLEMS AT TIMES.
MELCHESTER ROVERS
RACE
14
AND THAT WAS A **REAL** FINISHER'S GOAL FROM THE LOCAL LAD!
HAH! ALL ABOUT THE CROSS, RACE!
ABSOLUTELY.
AND ME TELLING YOU WHERE TO PUT IT.
OI!
hummel
LUCKY, ROY.
IF YOU SAY SO.
FINE BY ME. KEEP BEING LUCKY.
WHEEEEEEEEEEP
THAT'S IT, BOYS.
AND THAT'S THE END HERE. IT'S BEEN A VALIANT EFFORT BUT MELCHESTER HAVE NOW LOST THEIR FIRST **FIVE** GAMES OF THE SEASON.
IT SEEMS LIKE RELEGATION IS AN INEVITABILITY AT THIS POINT. BUT DOES THIS 4-1 DEFEAT PROVIDE SOME HOPE FOR THE FUTURE?

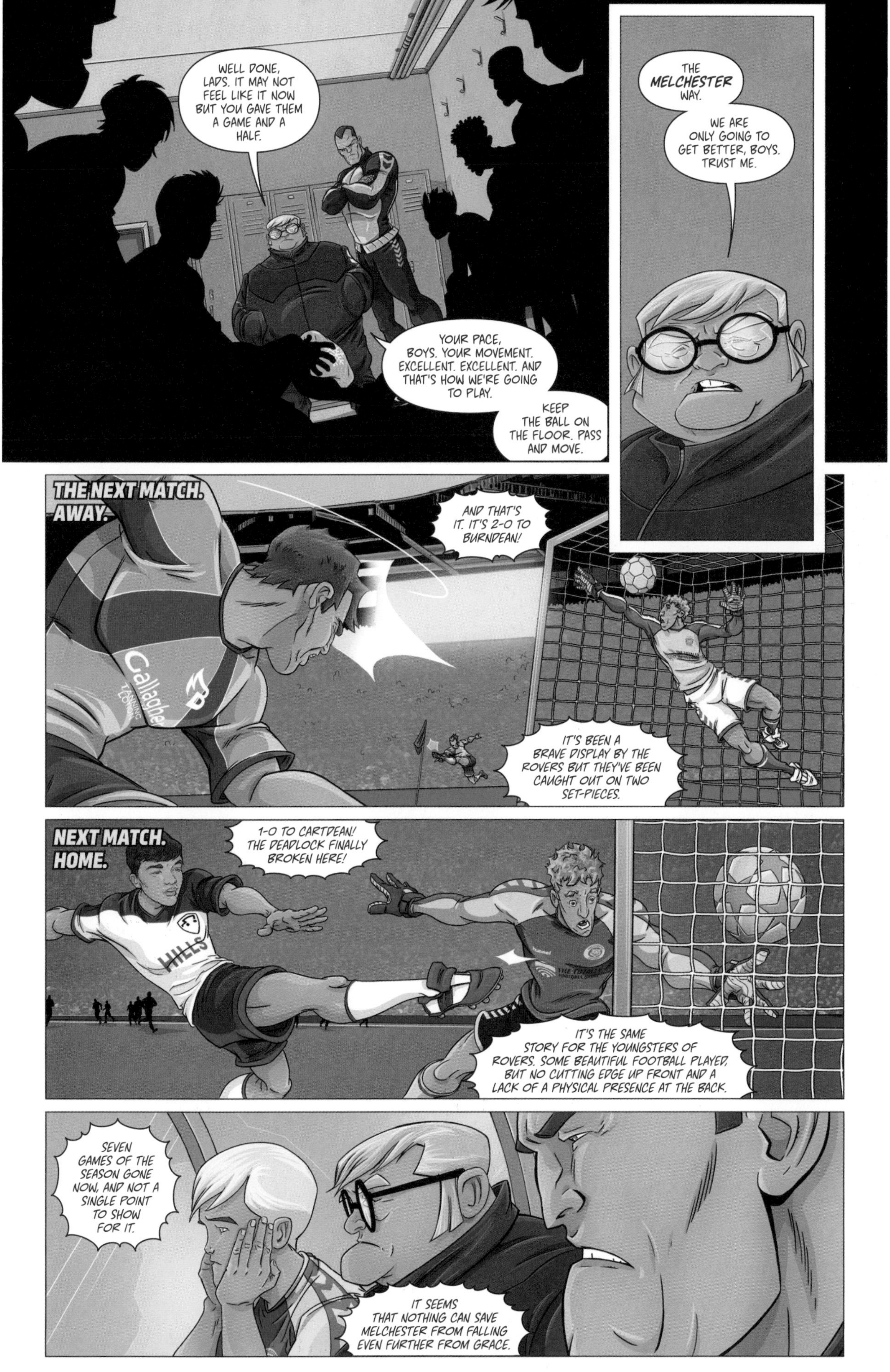
WELL DONE, LADS. IT MAY NOT FEEL LIKE IT NOW BUT YOU GAVE THEM A GAME AND A HALF.
YOUR PACE, BOYS. YOUR MOVEMENT. EXCELLENT. EXCELLENT. AND THAT'S HOW WE'RE GOING TO PLAY.
KEEP THE BALL ON THE FLOOR. PASS AND MOVE.
THE MELCHESTER WAY.
WE ARE ONLY GOING TO GET BETTER, BOYS. TRUST ME.
THE NEXT MATCH. AWAY.
AND THAT'S IT. IT'S 2-0 TO BURNDEAN!
IT'S BEEN A BRAVE DISPLAY BY THE ROVERS BUT THEY'VE BEEN CAUGHT OUT ON TWO SET-PIECES.
NEXT MATCH. HOME.
1-0 TO CARTDEAN! THE DEADLOCK FINALLY BROKEN HERE!
IT'S THE SAME STORY FOR THE YOUNGSTERS OF ROVERS. SOME BEAUTIFUL FOOTBALL PLAYED, BUT NO CUTTING EDGE UP FRONT AND A LACK OF A PHYSICAL PRESENCE AT THE BACK.
SEVEN GAMES OF THE SEASON GONE NOW, AND NOT A SINGLE POINT TO SHOW FOR IT.
IT SEEMS THAT NOTHING CAN SAVE MELCHESTER FROM FALLING EVEN FURTHER FROM GRACE.

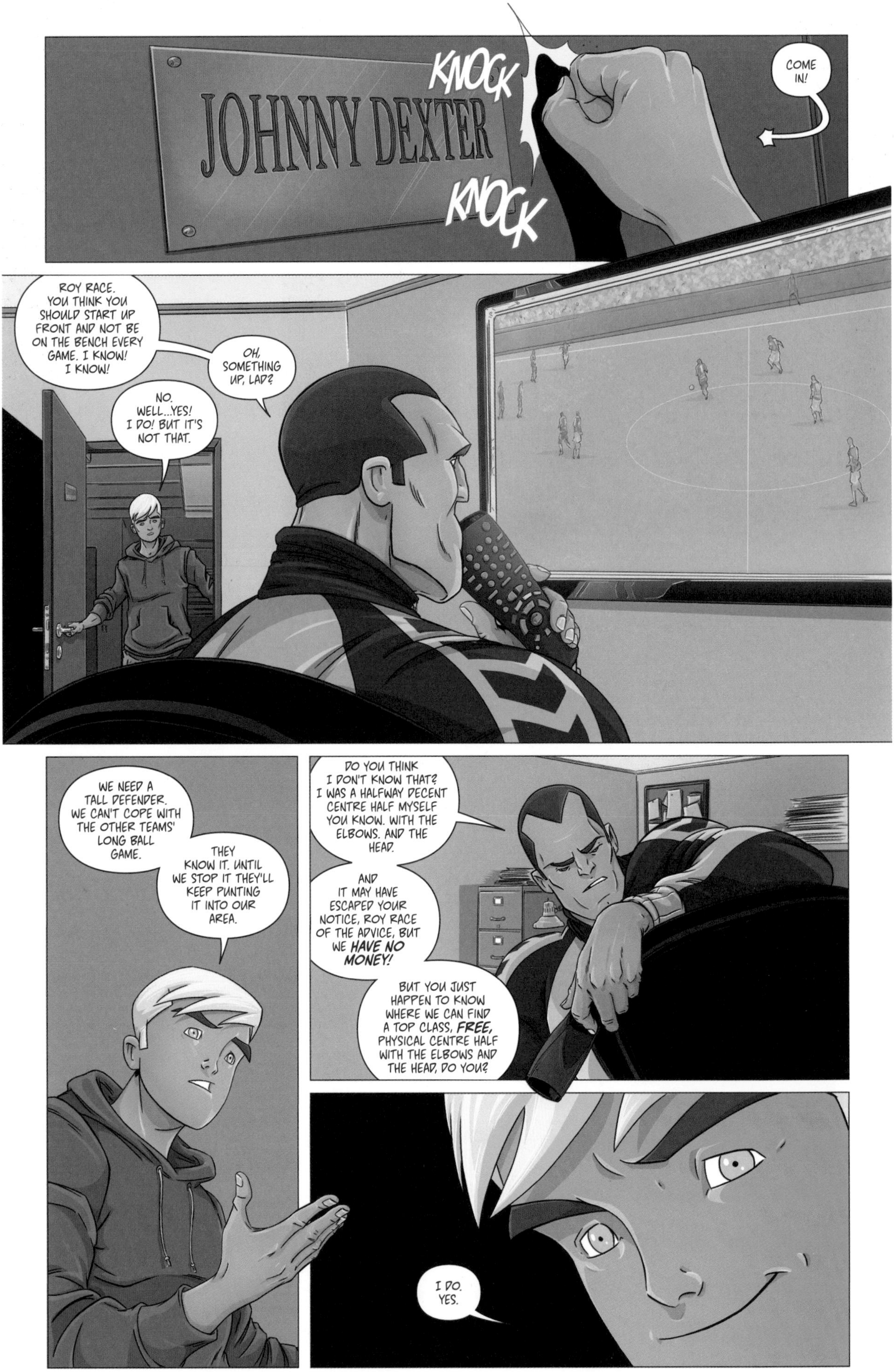
JOHNNY DEXTER
KNOCK
KNOCK
COME IN!
ROY RACE. YOU THINK YOU SHOULD START UP FRONT AND NOT BE ON THE BENCH EVERY GAME. I KNOW! I KNOW!
OH, SOMETHING UP, LAD?
NO. WELL...YES! I DO! BUT IT'S NOT THAT.
WE NEED A TALL DEFENDER. WE CAN'T COPE WITH THE OTHER TEAMS' LONG BALL GAME.
THEY KNOW IT. UNTIL WE STOP IT THEY'LL KEEP PUNTING IT INTO OUR AREA.
DO YOU THINK I DON'T KNOW THAT? I WAS A HALFWAY DECENT CENTRE HALF MYSELF YOU KNOW. WITH THE ELBOWS. AND THE HEAD.
AND IT MAY HAVE ESCAPED YOUR NOTICE, ROY RACE OF THE ADVICE, BUT WE HAVE NO MONEY!
BUT YOU JUST HAPPEN TO KNOW WHERE WE CAN FIND A TOP CLASS, FREE, PHYSICAL CENTRE HALF WITH THE ELBOWS AND THE HEAD, DO YOU?
I DO. YES.

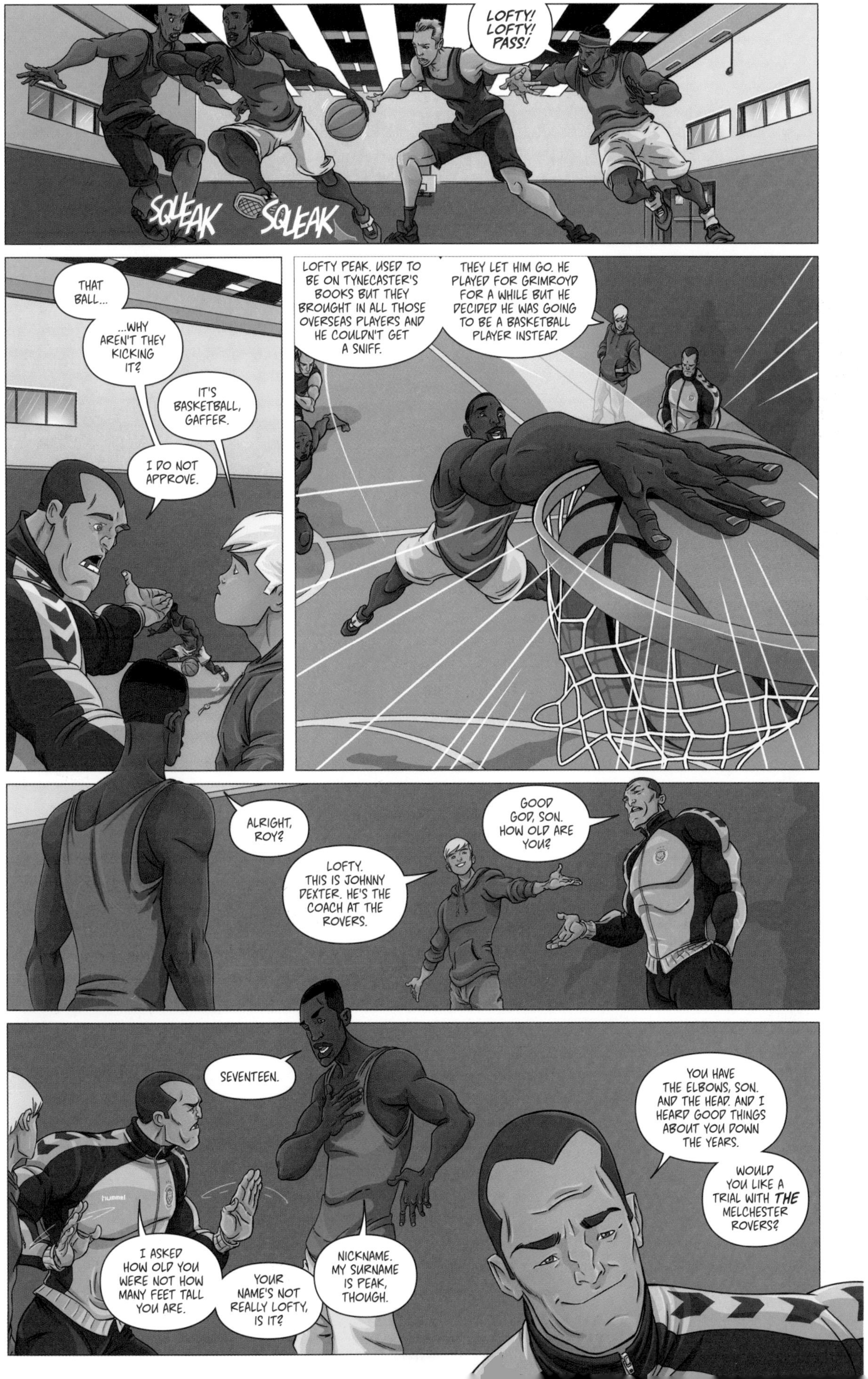
LOFTY! LOFTY! PASS!
SQUEAK SQUEAK
THAT BALL...
...WHY AREN'T THEY KICKING IT?
IT'S BASKETBALL, GAFFER.
I DO NOT APPROVE.
LOFTY PEAK. USED TO BE ON TYNECASTER'S BOOKS BUT THEY BROUGHT IN ALL THOSE OVERSEAS PLAYERS AND HE COULDN'T GET A SNIFF.
THEY LET HIM GO. HE PLAYED FOR GRIMROYD FOR A WHILE BUT HE DECIDED HE WAS GOING TO BE A BASKETBALL PLAYER INSTEAD.
ALRIGHT, ROY?
LOFTY. THIS IS JOHNNY DEXTER. HE'S THE COACH AT THE ROVERS.
GOOD GOD, SON. HOW OLD ARE YOU?
SEVENTEEN.
I ASKED HOW OLD YOU WERE NOT HOW MANY FEET TALL YOU ARE.
YOUR NAME'S NOT REALLY LOFTY, IS IT?
NICKNAME. MY SURNAME IS PEAK, THOUGH.
YOU HAVE THE ELBOWS, SON. AND THE HEAD. AND I HEARD GOOD THINGS ABOUT YOU DOWN THE YEARS.
WOULD YOU LIKE A TRIAL WITH *THE* MELCHESTER ROVERS?

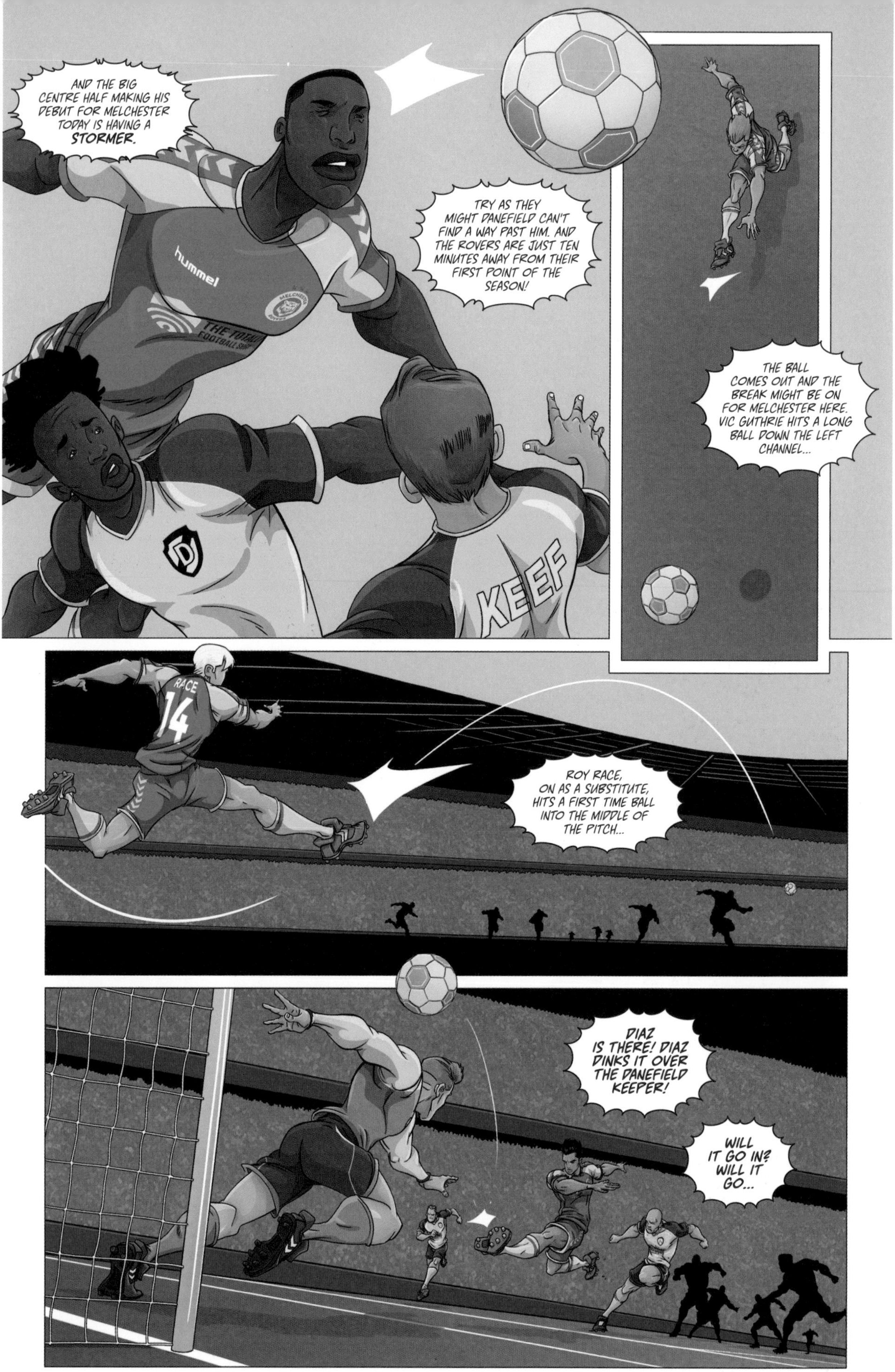
AND THE BIG CENTRE HALF MAKING HIS DEBUT FOR MELCHESTER TODAY IS HAVING A STORMER.
TRY AS THEY MIGHT DANEFIELD CAN'T FIND A WAY PAST HIM. AND THE ROVERS ARE JUST TEN MINUTES AWAY FROM THEIR FIRST POINT OF THE SEASON!
KEEF
THE BALL COMES OUT AND THE BREAK MIGHT BE ON FOR MELCHESTER HERE. VIC GUTHRIE HITS A LONG BALL DOWN THE LEFT CHANNEL...
RACE 14
ROY RACE, ON AS A SUBSTITUTE, HITS A FIRST TIME BALL INTO THE MIDDLE OF THE PITCH...
DIAZ IS THERE! DIAZ DINKS IT OVER THE DANEFIELD KEEPER!
WILL IT GO IN? WILL IT GO...

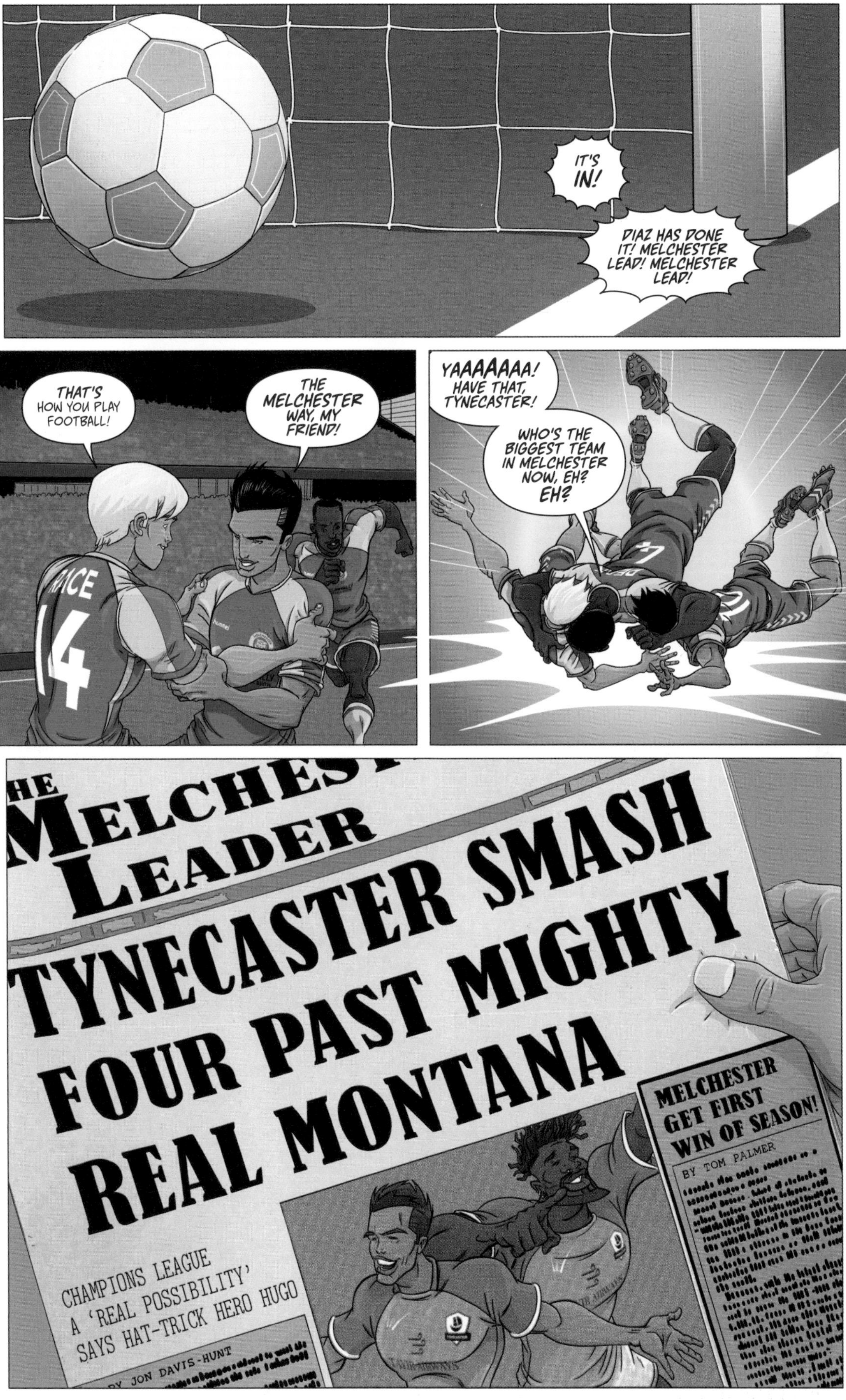
IT'S IN!
DIAZ HAS DONE IT! MELCHESTER LEAD! MELCHESTER LEAD!
THAT'S HOW YOU PLAY FOOTBALL!
THE MELCHESTER WAY, MY FRIEND!
YAAAAAAA! HAVE THAT, TYNECASTER!
WHO'S THE BIGGEST TEAM IN MELCHESTER NOW, EH? EH?
LEADER
TYNECASTER SMASH FOUR PAST MIGHTY REAL MONTANA
MELCHESTER GET FIRST WIN OF SEASON!
BY TOM PALMER
CHAMPIONS LEAGUE A 'REAL POSSIBILITY' SAYS HAT-TRICK HERO HUGO
BY JON DAVIS-HUNT

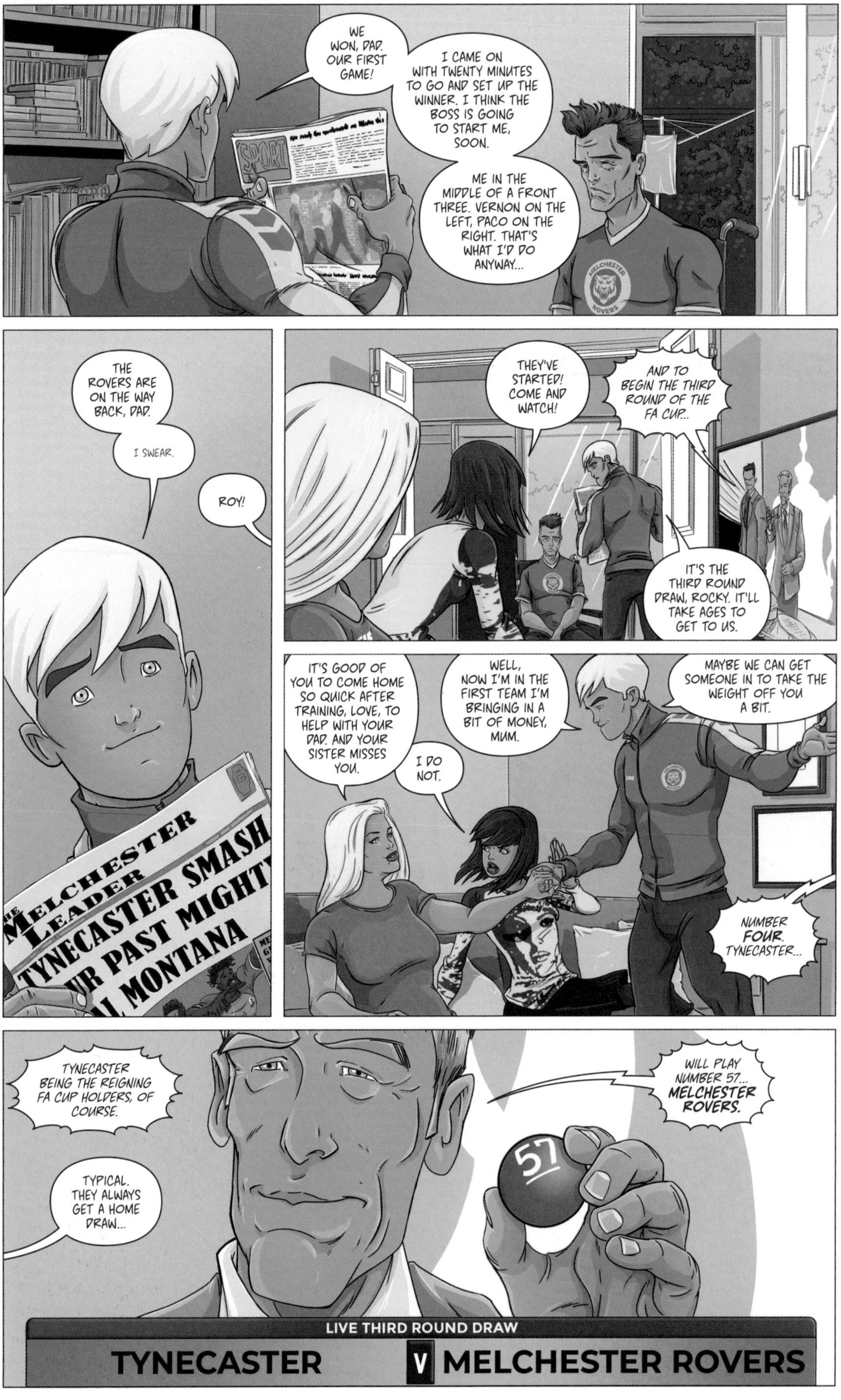
SPORT
WE WON, DAD. OUR FIRST GAME!
I CAME ON WITH TWENTY MINUTES TO GO AND SET UP THE WINNER. I THINK THE BOSS IS GOING TO START ME, SOON.
ME IN THE MIDDLE OF A FRONT THREE. VERNON ON THE LEFT, PACO ON THE RIGHT. THAT'S WHAT I'D DO ANYWAY...
THE ROVERS ARE ON THE WAY BACK, DAD.
I SWEAR.
ROY!
MELCHESTER LEADER
TYNECASTER SMASH
THEY'VE STARTED! COME AND WATCH!
AND TO BEGIN THE THIRD ROUND OF THE FA CUP...
IT'S THE THIRD ROUND DRAW, ROCKY. IT'LL TAKE AGES TO GET TO US.
IT'S GOOD OF YOU TO COME HOME SO QUICK AFTER TRAINING, LOVE, TO HELP WITH YOUR DAD. AND YOUR SISTER MISSES YOU.
I DO NOT.
WELL, NOW I'M IN THE FIRST TEAM I'M BRINGING IN A BIT OF MONEY, MUM.
MAYBE WE CAN GET SOMEONE IN TO TAKE THE WEIGHT OFF YOU A BIT.
NUMBER FOUR. TYNECASTER...
TYNECASTER BEING THE REIGNING FA CUP HOLDERS, OF COURSE.
TYPICAL. THEY ALWAYS GET A HOME DRAW...
WILL PLAY NUMBER 57... MELCHESTER ROVERS.
57
LIVE THIRD ROUND DRAW
TYNECASTER V MELCHESTER ROVERS

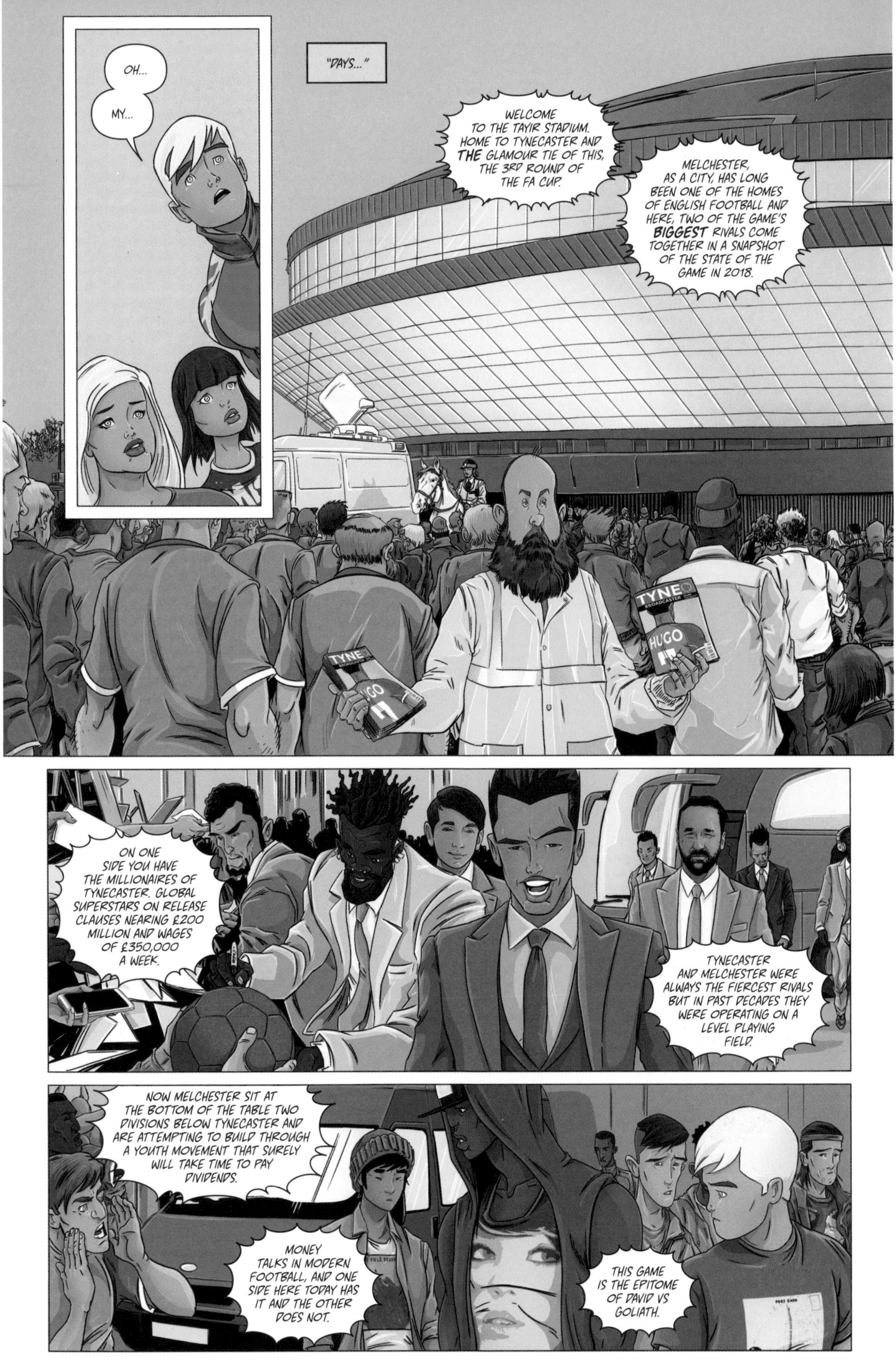
OH...
MY...
"DAYS..."
WELCOME TO THE TAYIR STADIUM. HOME TO TYNECASTER AND **THE** GLAMOUR TIE OF THIS, THE 3RD ROUND OF THE FA CUP.
MELCHESTER, AS A CITY, HAS LONG BEEN ONE OF THE HOMES OF ENGLISH FOOTBALL AND HERE, TWO OF THE GAME'S **BIGGEST** RIVALS COME TOGETHER IN A SNAPSHOT OF THE STATE OF THE GAME IN 2018.
TYNE
BROADCASTER
HUGO
ON ONE SIDE YOU HAVE THE MILLIONAIRES OF TYNECASTER. GLOBAL SUPERSTARS ON RELEASE CLAUSES NEARING £200 MILLION AND WAGES OF £350,000 A WEEK.
TYNECASTER AND MELCHESTER WERE ALWAYS THE FIERCEST RIVALS BUT IN PAST DECADES THEY WERE OPERATING ON A LEVEL PLAYING FIELD.
NOW MELCHESTER SIT AT THE BOTTOM OF THE TABLE TWO DIVISIONS BELOW TYNECASTER AND ARE ATTEMPTING TO BUILD THROUGH A YOUTH MOVEMENT THAT SURELY WILL TAKE TIME TO PAY DIVIDENDS.
MONEY TALKS IN MODERN FOOTBALL, AND ONE SIDE HERE TODAY HAS IT AND THE OTHER DOES NOT.
THIS GAME IS THE EPITOME OF DAVID VS GOLIATH.

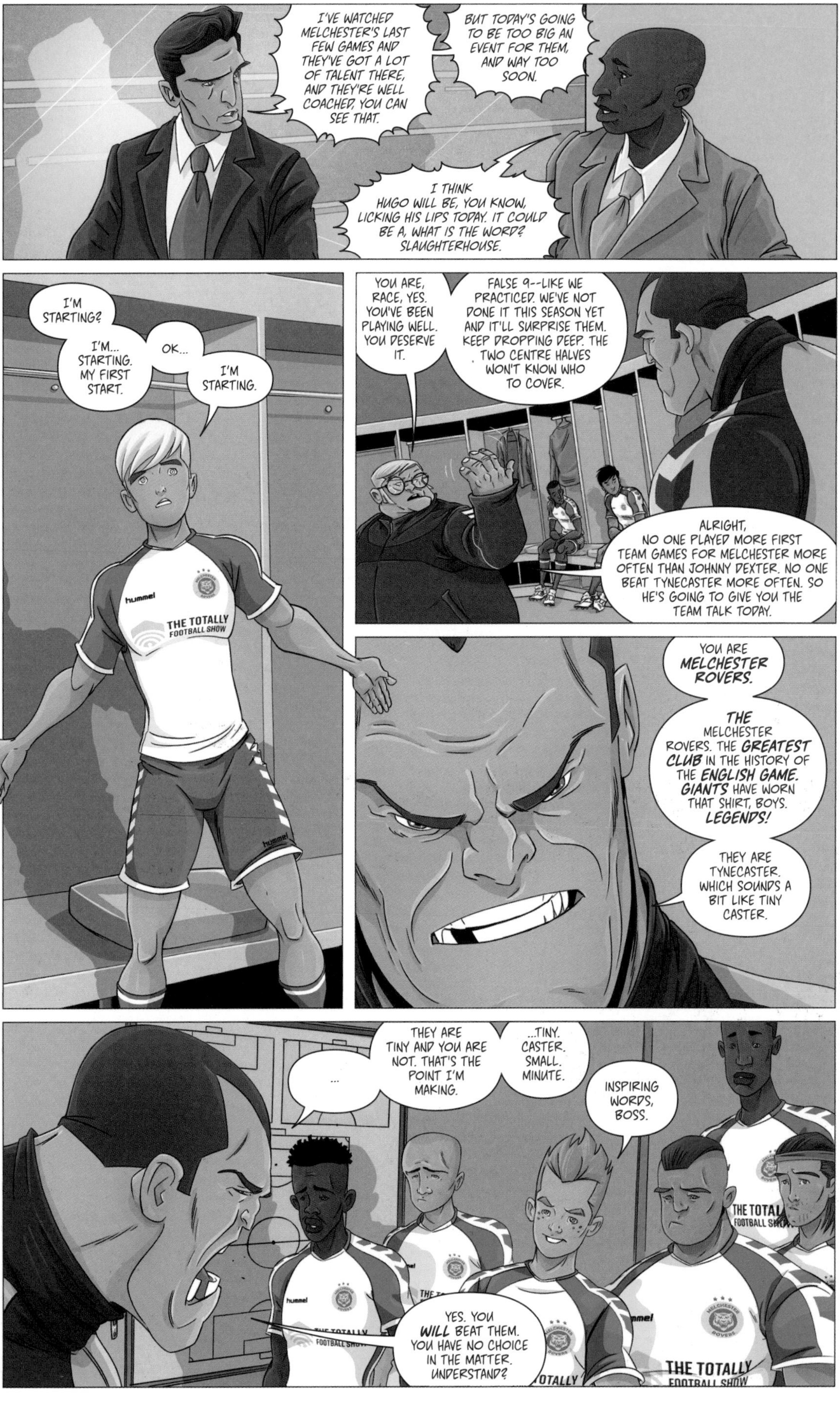
I'VE WATCHED MELCHESTER'S LAST FEW GAMES AND THEY'VE GOT A LOT OF TALENT THERE, AND THEY'RE WELL COACHED, YOU CAN SEE THAT.
BUT TODAY'S GOING TO BE TOO BIG AN EVENT FOR THEM, AND WAY TOO SOON.
I THINK HUGO WILL BE, YOU KNOW, LICKING HIS LIPS TODAY. IT COULD BE A, WHAT IS THE WORD? SLAUGHTERHOUSE.
I'M STARTING?
I'M... STARTING. MY FIRST START.
OK...
I'M STARTING.
YOU ARE, RACE, YES. YOU'VE BEEN PLAYING WELL. YOU DESERVE IT.
FALSE 9--LIKE WE PRACTICED. WE'VE NOT DONE IT THIS SEASON YET AND IT'LL SURPRISE THEM. KEEP DROPPING DEEP. THE TWO CENTRE HALVES WON'T KNOW WHO TO COVER.
ALRIGHT, NO ONE PLAYED MORE FIRST TEAM GAMES FOR MELCHESTER MORE OFTEN THAN JOHNNY DEXTER. NO ONE BEAT TYNECASTER MORE OFTEN. SO HE'S GOING TO GIVE YOU THE TEAM TALK TODAY.
YOU ARE MELCHESTER ROVERS.
THE MELCHESTER ROVERS. THE GREATEST CLUB IN THE HISTORY OF THE ENGLISH GAME. GIANTS HAVE WORN THAT SHIRT, BOYS. LEGENDS!
THEY ARE TYNECASTER. WHICH SOUNDS A BIT LIKE TINY CASTER.
...
THEY ARE TINY AND YOU ARE NOT. THAT'S THE POINT I'M MAKING.
...TINY. CASTER. SMALL. MINUTE.
INSPIRING WORDS, BOSS.
YES. YOU WILL BEAT THEM. YOU HAVE NO CHOICE IN THE MATTER. UNDERSTAND?

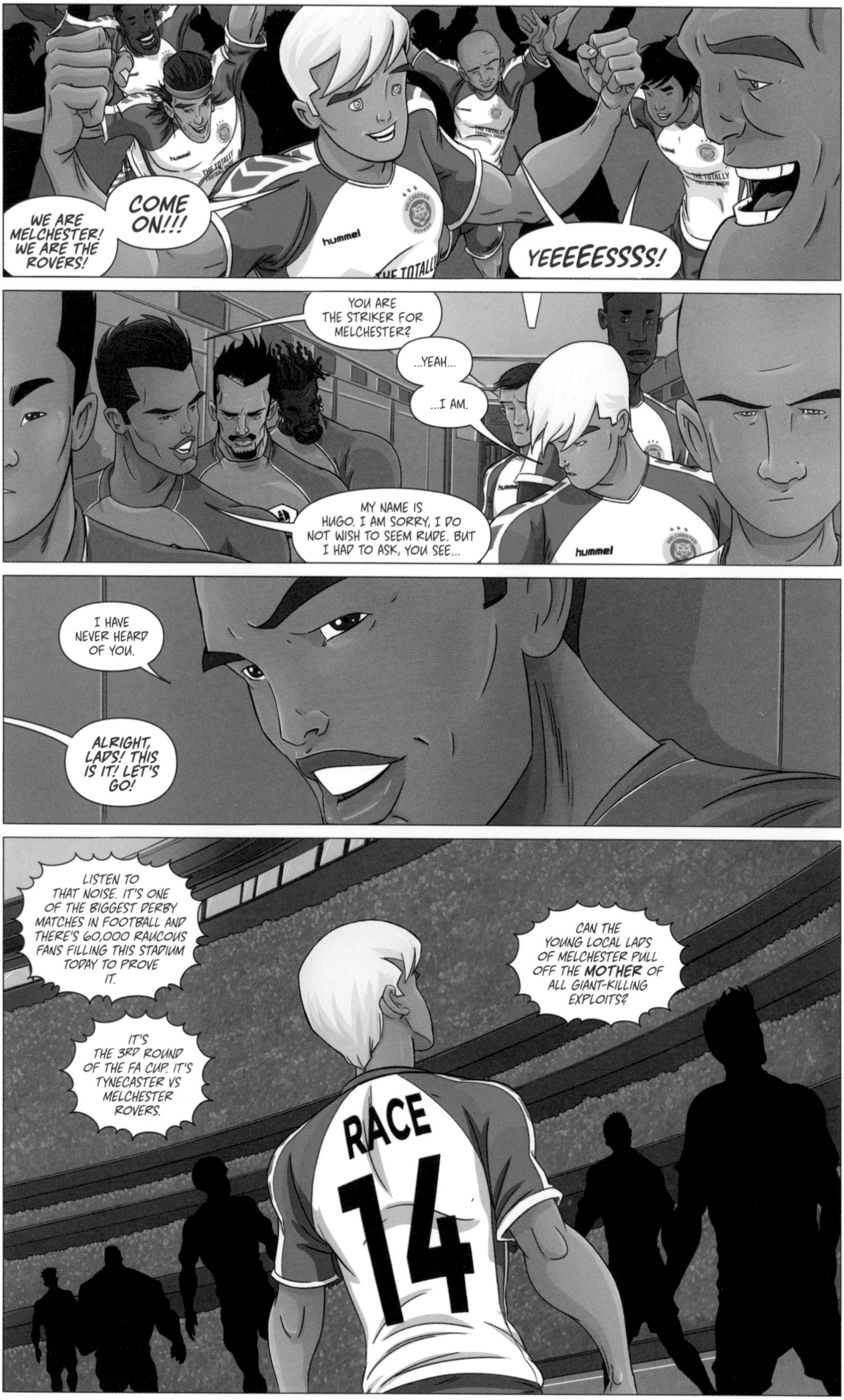
WE ARE MELCHESTER! WE ARE THE ROVERS!
COME ON!!!
YEEEEESSSS!
YOU ARE THE STRIKER FOR MELCHESTER?
...YEAH...
...I AM.
MY NAME IS HUGO. I AM SORRY, I DO NOT WISH TO SEEM RUDE. BUT I HAD TO ASK, YOU SEE...
I HAVE NEVER HEARD OF YOU.
ALRIGHT, LADS! THIS IS IT! LET'S GO!
LISTEN TO THAT NOISE. IT'S ONE OF THE BIGGEST DERBY MATCHES IN FOOTBALL AND THERE'S 60,000 RAUCOUS FANS FILLING THIS STADIUM TODAY TO PROVE IT.
IT'S THE 3RD ROUND OF THE FA CUP. IT'S TYNECASTER VS MELCHESTER ROVERS.
CAN THE YOUNG LOCAL LADS OF MELCHESTER PULL OFF THE **MOTHER** OF ALL GIANT-KILLING EXPLOITS?
RACE
14

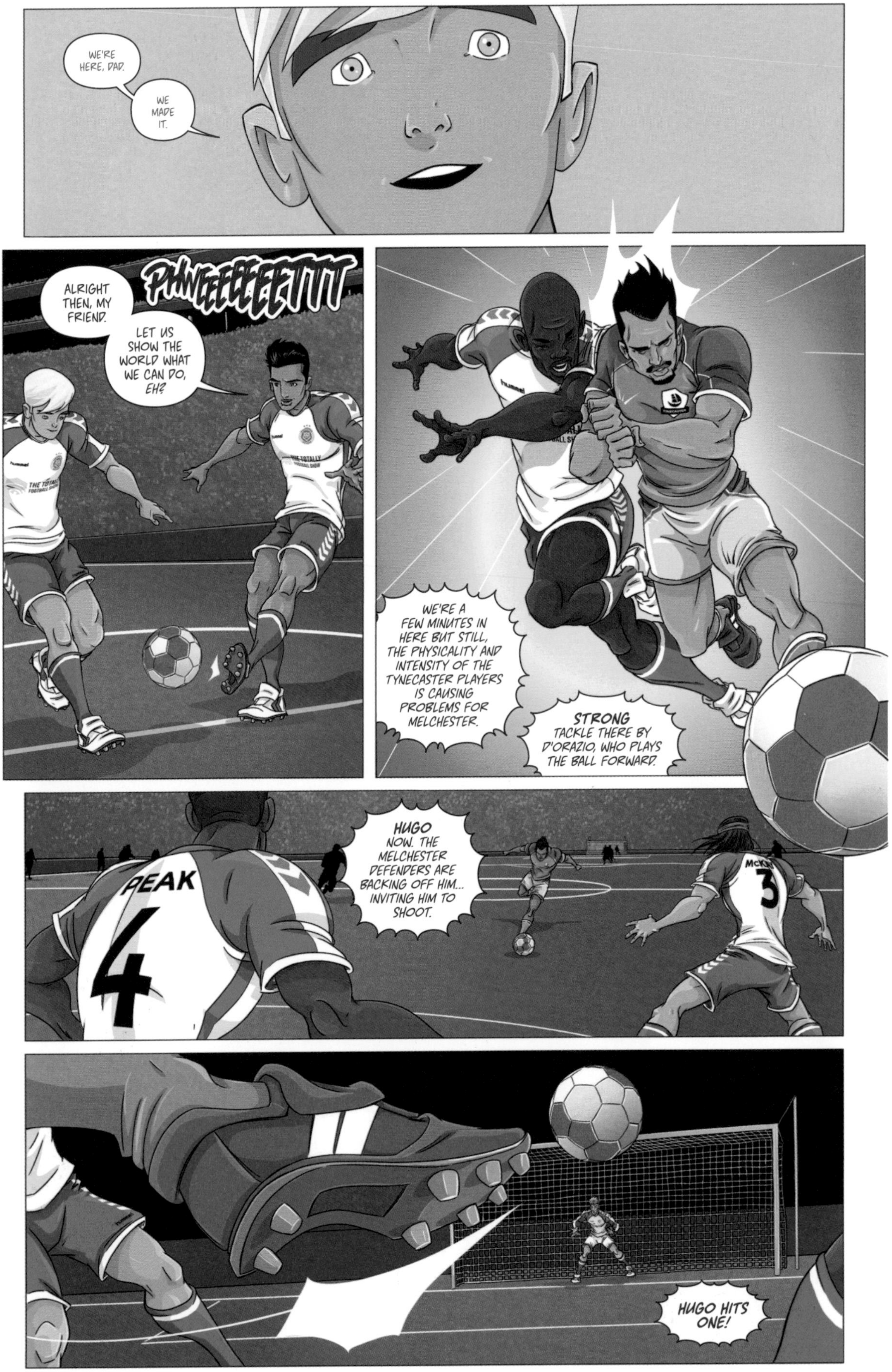

WE'RE HERE, DAD.
WE MADE IT.
PHWEEEEEEETTTT
ALRIGHT THEN, MY FRIEND.
LET US SHOW THE WORLD WHAT WE CAN DO, EH?
WE'RE A FEW MINUTES IN HERE BUT STILL, THE PHYSICALITY AND INTENSITY OF THE TYNECASTER PLAYERS IS CAUSING PROBLEMS FOR MELCHESTER.
STRONG TACKLE THERE BY D'ORAZIO, WHO PLAYS THE BALL FORWARD.
PEAK
4
HUGO NOW. THE MELCHESTER DEFENDERS ARE BACKING OFF HIM... INVITING HIM TO SHOOT.
3
HUGO HITS ONE!

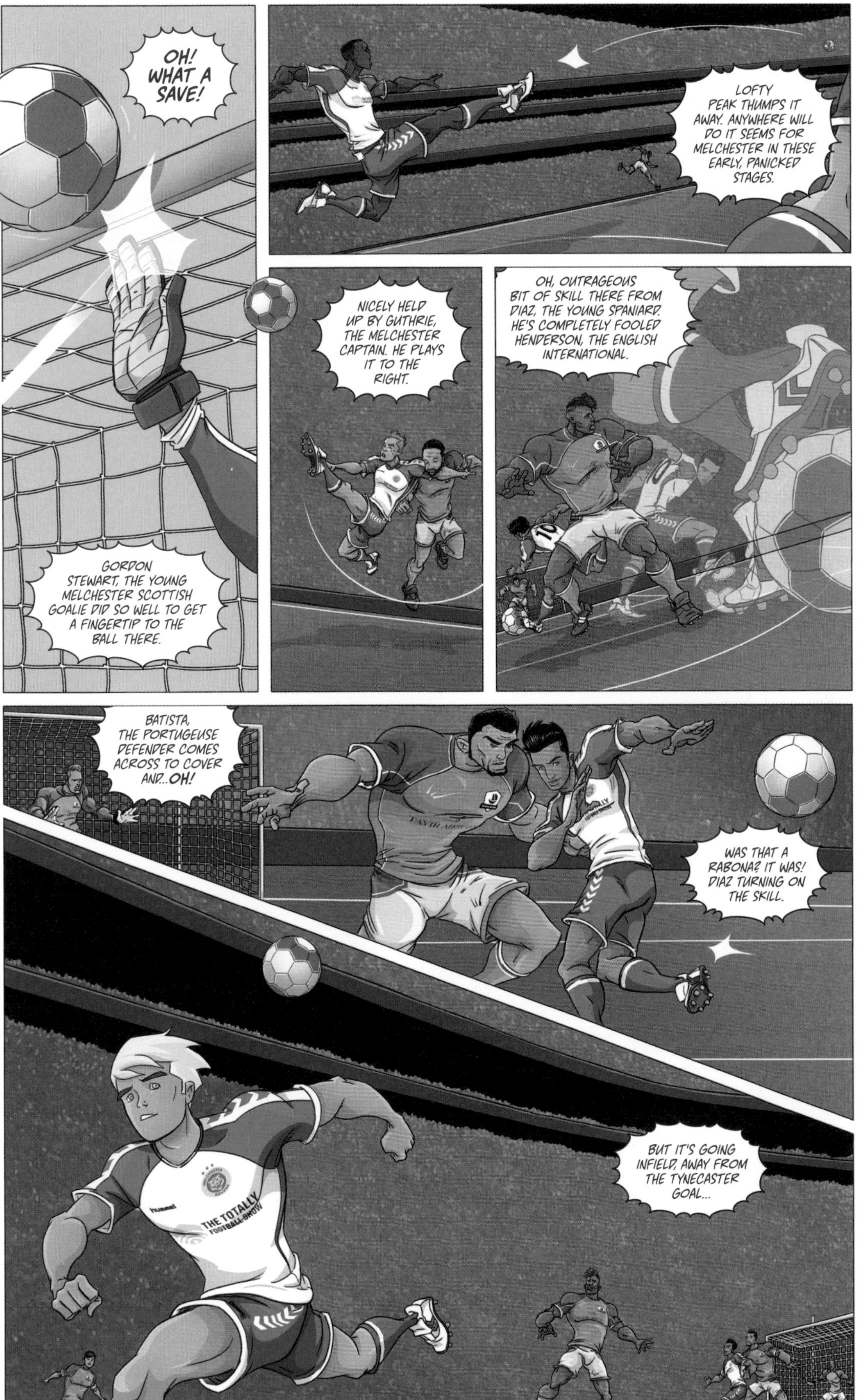
OH! WHAT A SAVE!
GORDON STEWART, THE YOUNG MELCHESTER SCOTTISH GOALIE DID SO WELL TO GET A FINGERTIP TO THE BALL THERE.
LOFTY PEAK THUMPS IT AWAY. ANYWHERE WILL DO IT SEEMS FOR MELCHESTER IN THESE EARLY, PANICKED STAGES.
NICELY HELD UP BY GUTHRIE, THE MELCHESTER CAPTAIN. HE PLAYS IT TO THE RIGHT.
OH, OUTRAGEOUS BIT OF SKILL THERE FROM DIAZ, THE YOUNG SPANIARD. HE'S COMPLETELY FOOLED HENDERSON, THE ENGLISH INTERNATIONAL.
BATISTA, THE PORTUGEUSE DEFENDER COMES ACROSS TO COVER AND...OH!
WAS THAT A RABONA? IT WAS! DIAZ TURNING ON THE SKILL.
BUT IT'S GOING INFIELD, AWAY FROM THE TYNECASTER GOAL...
THE TOTALLY FOOTBALL SHOW

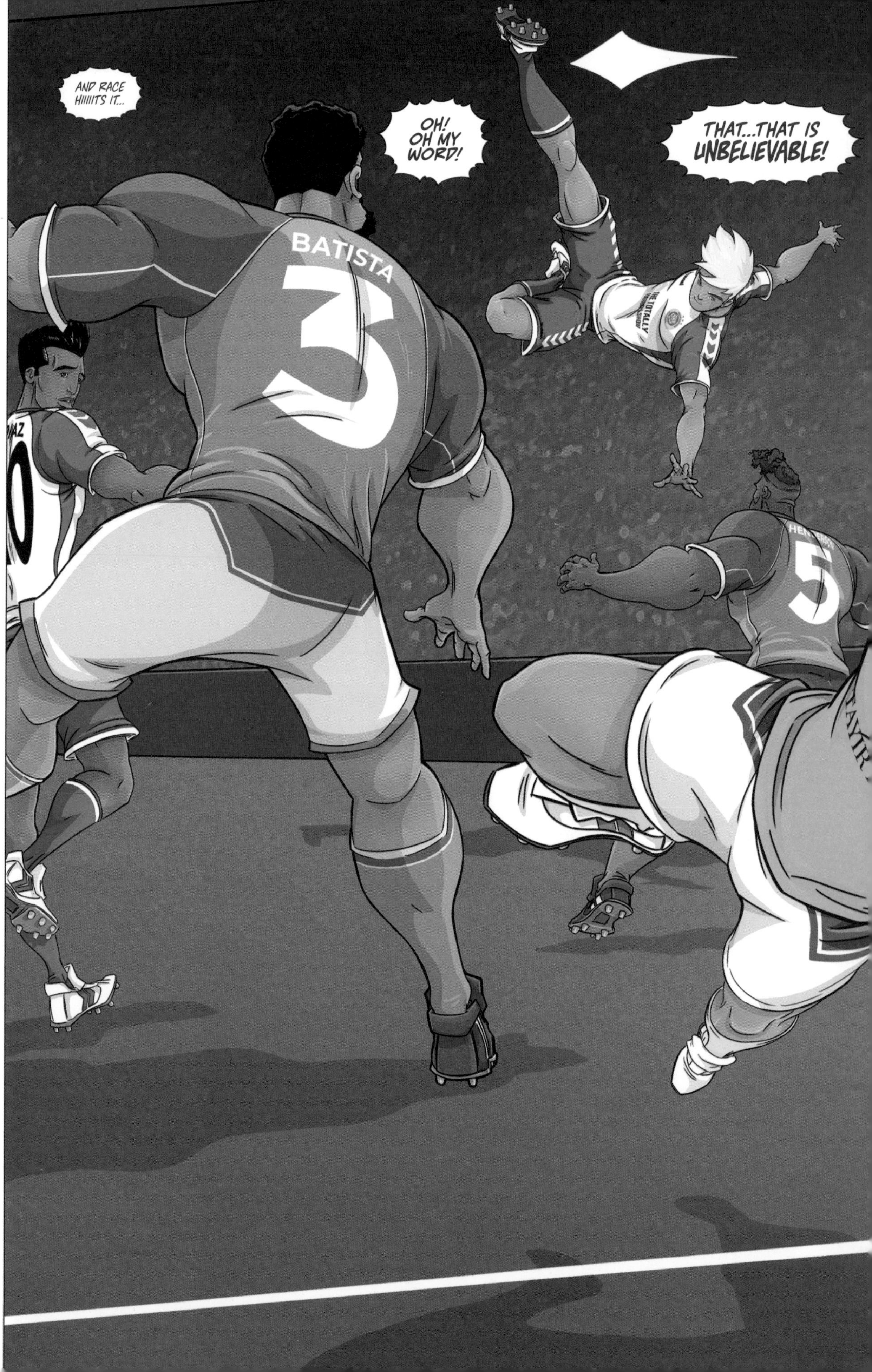
AND RACE HIIIIITS IT...
OH! OH MY WORD!
THAT...THAT IS UNBELIEVABLE!
BATISTA
3
HENDERSON
5

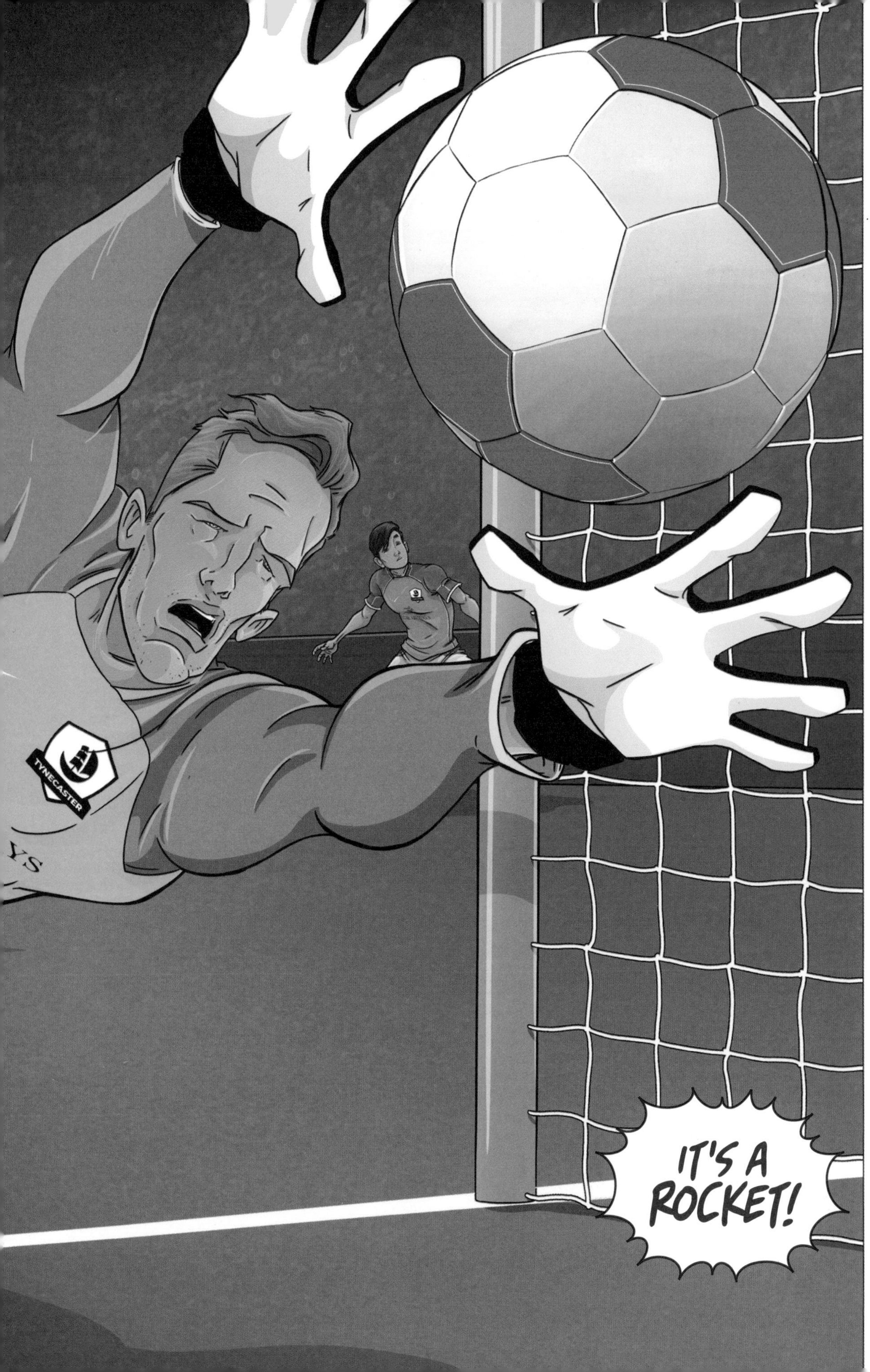
TYNECASTER
IT'S A ROCKET!

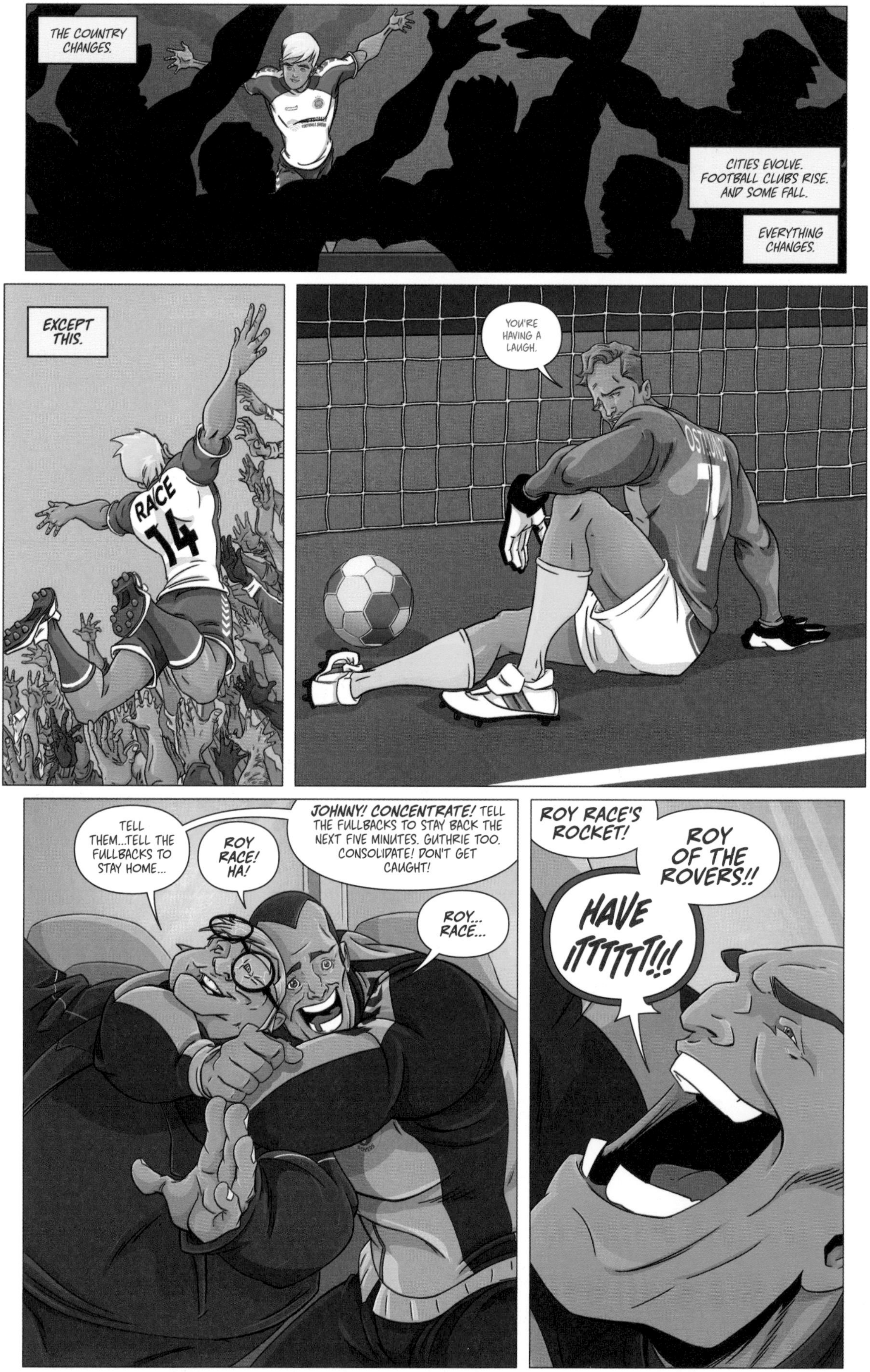
THE COUNTRY CHANGES.
CITIES EVOLVE. FOOTBALL CLUBS RISE. AND SOME FALL.
EVERYTHING CHANGES.
EXCEPT THIS.
RACE 14
YOU'RE HAVING A LAUGH.
TELL THEM...TELL THE FULLBACKS TO STAY HOME...
ROY RACE! HA!
JOHNNY! CONCENTRATE! TELL THE FULLBACKS TO STAY BACK THE NEXT FIVE MINUTES. GUTHRIE TOO. CONSOLIDATE! DON'T GET CAUGHT!
ROY... RACE...
ROY RACE'S ROCKET!
ROY OF THE ROVERS!!
HAVE IIIIIIT!!!

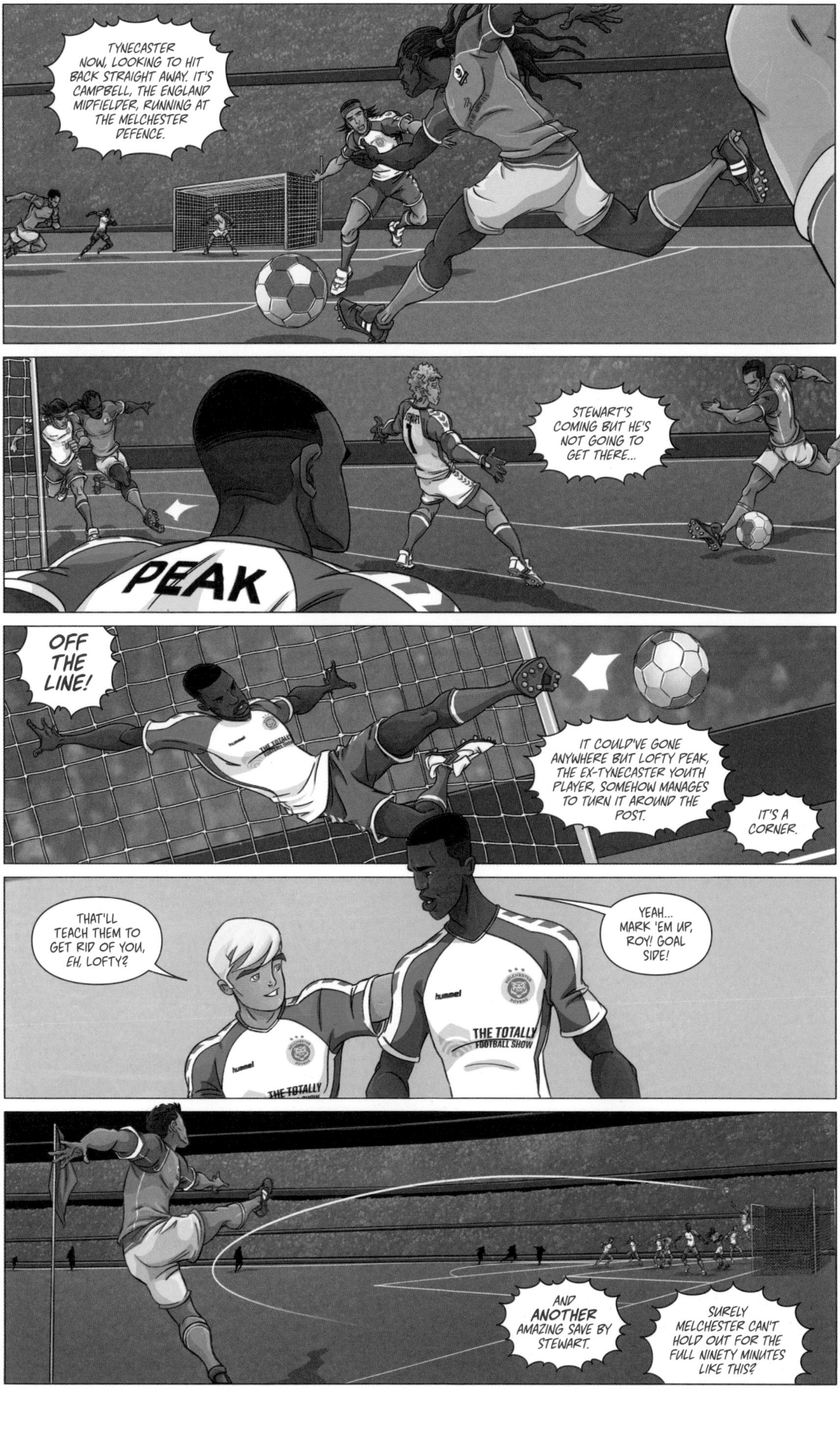
TYNECASTER NOW, LOOKING TO HIT BACK STRAIGHT AWAY. IT'S CAMPBELL, THE ENGLAND MIDFIELDER, RUNNING AT THE MELCHESTER DEFENCE.
STEWART'S COMING BUT HE'S NOT GOING TO GET THERE...
PEAK
OFF THE LINE!
IT COULD'VE GONE ANYWHERE BUT LOFTY PEAK, THE EX-TYNECASTER YOUTH PLAYER, SOMEHOW MANAGES TO TURN IT AROUND THE POST.
IT'S A CORNER.
THAT'LL TEACH THEM TO GET RID OF YOU, EH, LOFTY?
YEAH... MARK 'EM UP, ROY! GOAL SIDE!
AND **ANOTHER** AMAZING SAVE BY STEWART.
SURELY MELCHESTER CAN'T HOLD OUT FOR THE FULL NINETY MINUTES LIKE THIS?

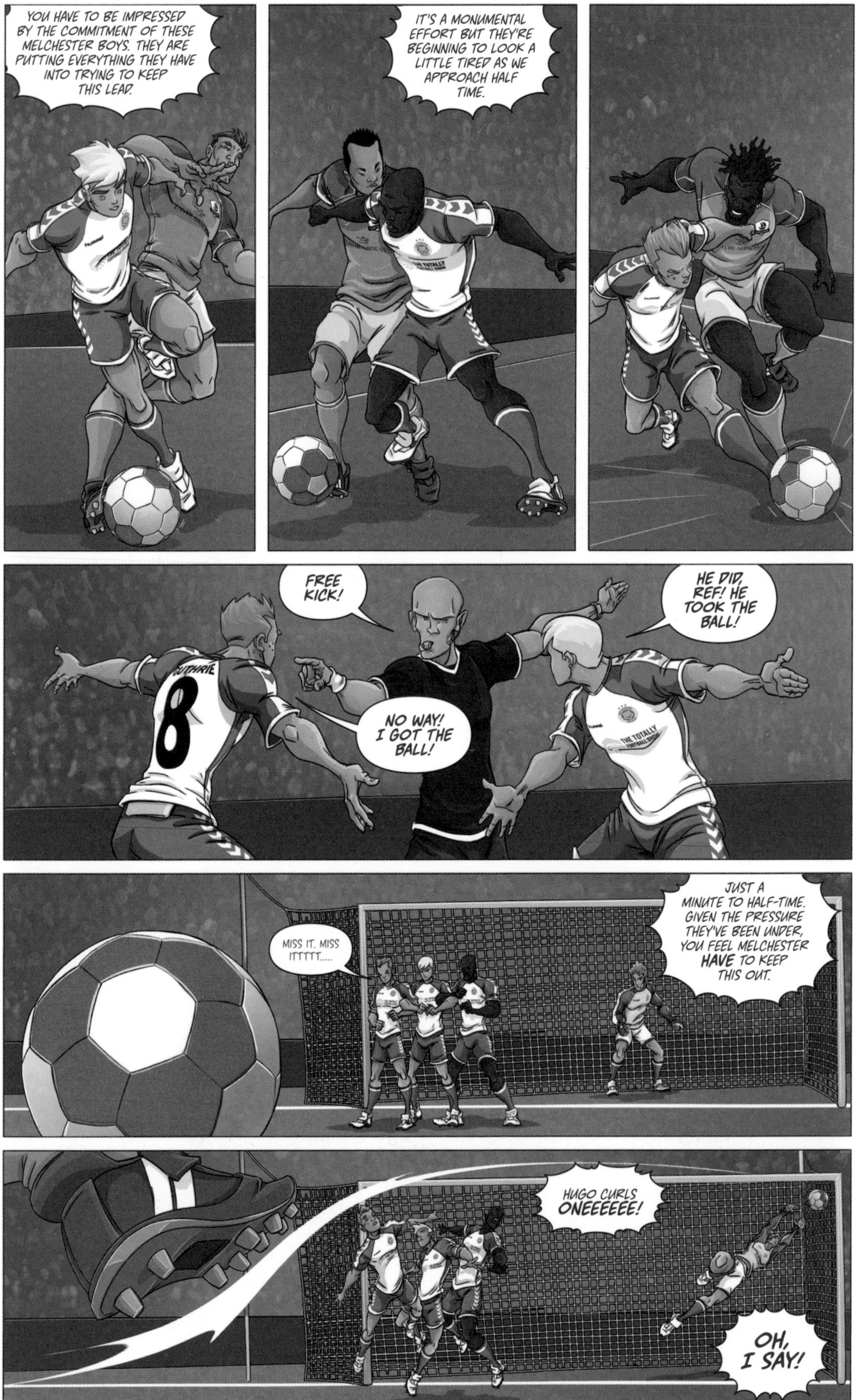
YOU HAVE TO BE IMPRESSED BY THE COMMITMENT OF THESE MELCHESTER BOYS. THEY ARE PUTTING EVERYTHING THEY HAVE INTO TRYING TO KEEP THIS LEAD.
IT'S A MONUMENTAL EFFORT BUT THEY'RE BEGINNING TO LOOK A LITTLE TIRED AS WE APPROACH HALF TIME.
FREE KICK!
NO WAY! I GOT THE BALL!
HE DID, REF! HE TOOK THE BALL!
MISS IT. MISS ITTTTT.....
JUST A MINUTE TO HALF-TIME. GIVEN THE PRESSURE THEY'VE BEEN UNDER, YOU FEEL MELCHESTER HAVE TO KEEP THIS OUT.
HUGO CURLS ONEEEEEE!
OH, I SAY!

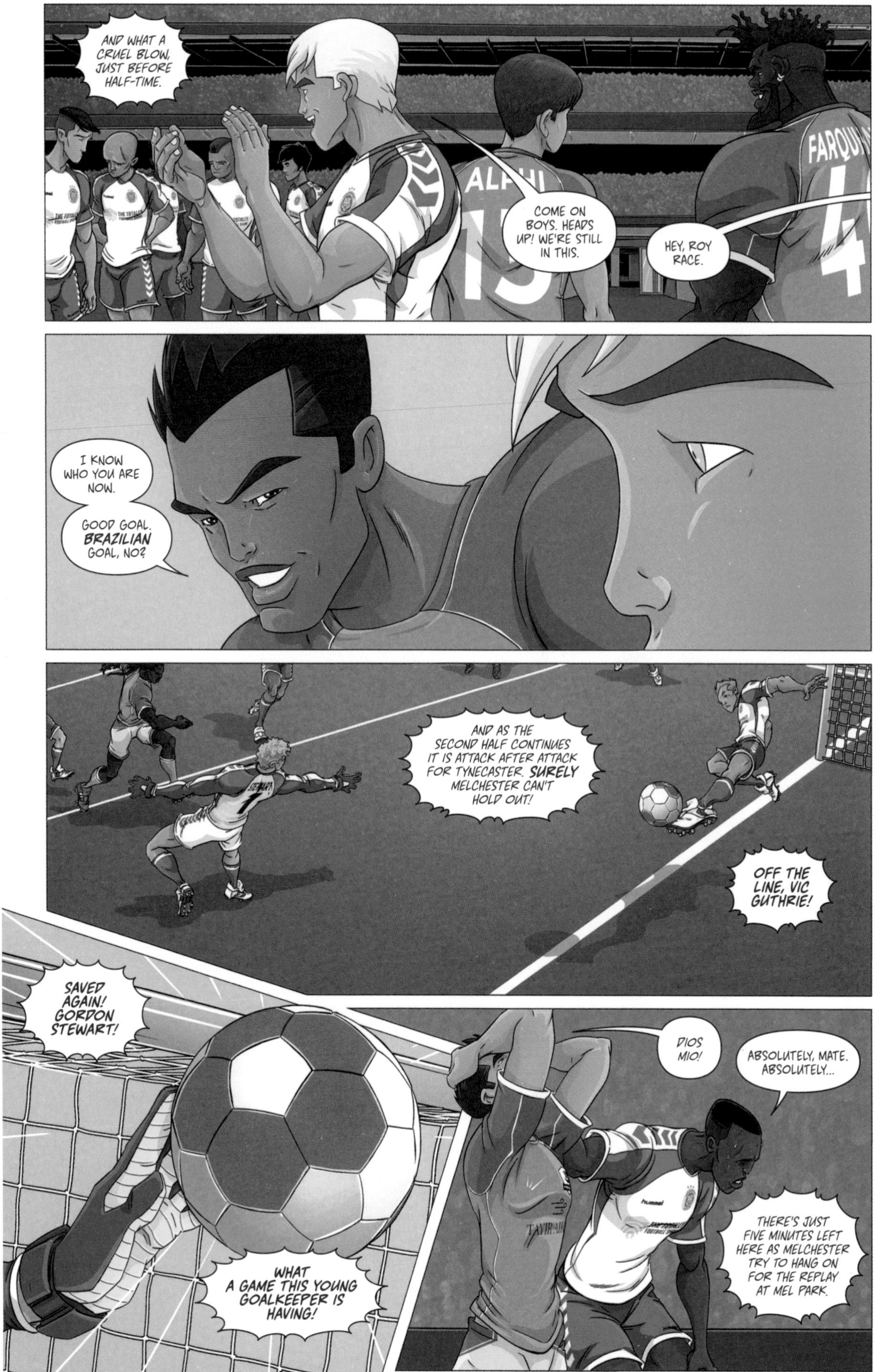
AND WHAT A CRUEL BLOW, JUST BEFORE HALF-TIME.
COME ON BOYS. HEADS UP! WE'RE STILL IN THIS.
HEY, ROY RACE.
ALFHI
15
FARQU
4
I KNOW WHO YOU ARE NOW.
GOOD GOAL. BRAZILIAN GOAL, NO?
AND AS THE SECOND HALF CONTINUES IT IS ATTACK AFTER ATTACK FOR TYNECASTER. SURELY MELCHESTER CAN'T HOLD OUT!
OFF THE LINE, VIC GUTHRIE!
SAVED AGAIN! GORDON STEWART!
DIOS MIO!
ABSOLUTELY, MATE. ABSOLUTELY...
WHAT A GAME THIS YOUNG GOALKEEPER IS HAVING!
THERE'S JUST FIVE MINUTES LEFT HERE AS MELCHESTER TRY TO HANG ON FOR THE REPLAY AT MEL PARK.

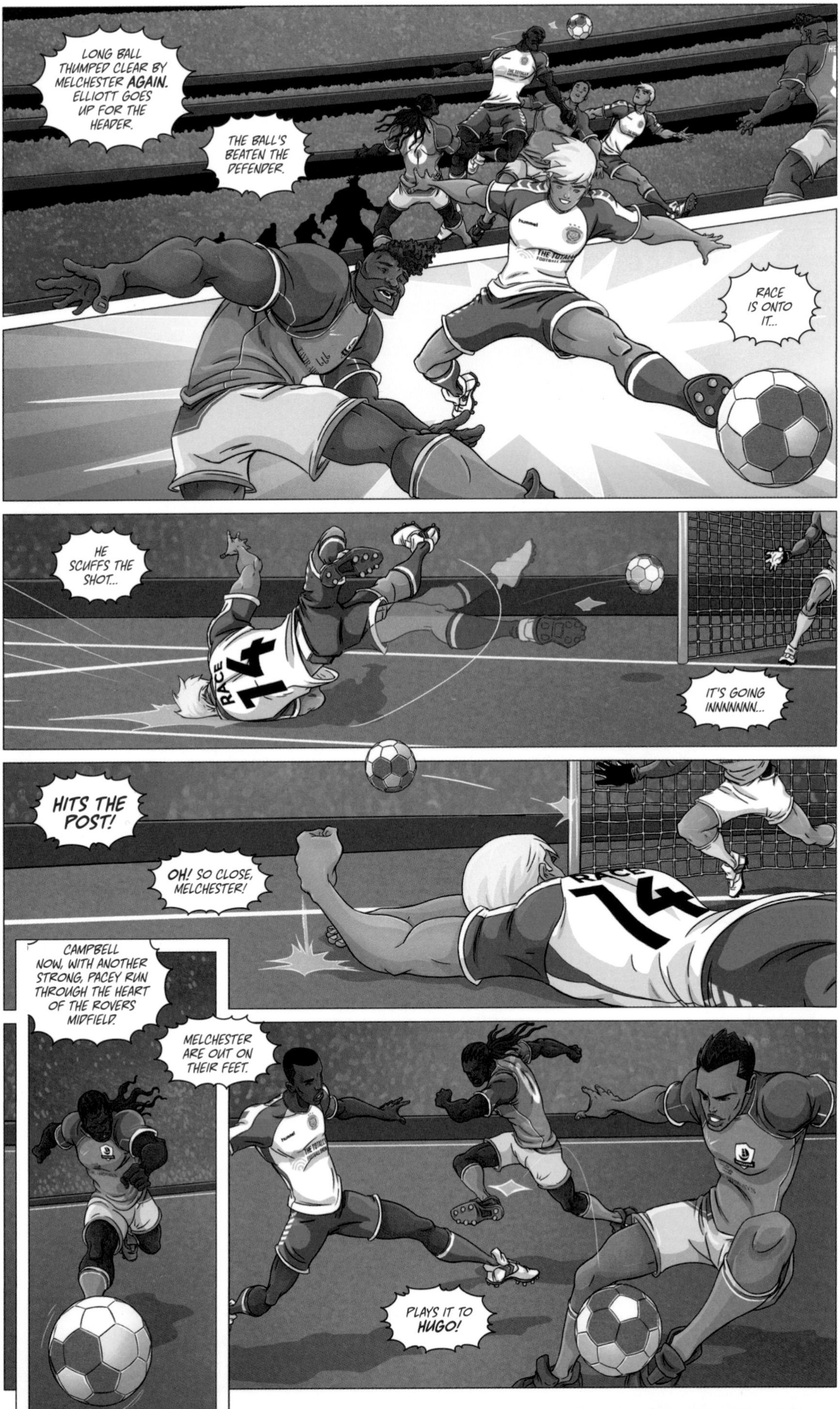
LONG BALL THUMPED CLEAR BY MELCHESTER AGAIN. ELLIOTT GOES UP FOR THE HEADER.
THE BALL'S BEATEN THE DEFENDER.
RACE IS ONTO IT...
HE SCUFFS THE SHOT...
RACE 14
IT'S GOING INNNNNNN...
HITS THE POST!
OH! SO CLOSE, MELCHESTER!
RACE 14
CAMPBELL NOW, WITH ANOTHER STRONG, PACEY RUN THROUGH THE HEART OF THE ROVERS MIDFIELD.
MELCHESTER ARE OUT ON THEIR FEET.
PLAYS IT TO HUGO!

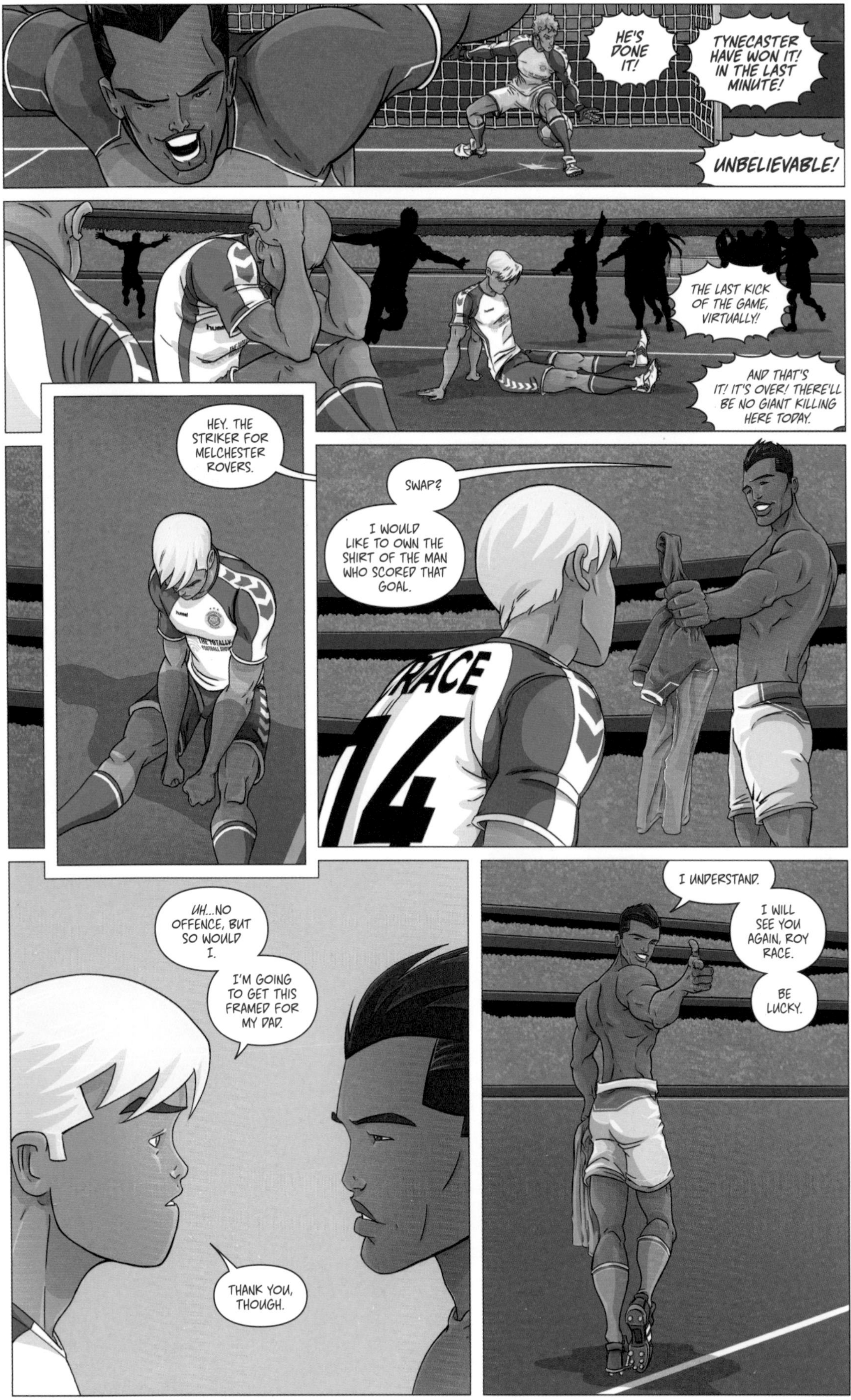
HE'S DONE IT!
TYNECASTER HAVE WON IT! IN THE LAST MINUTE!
UNBELIEVABLE!
THE LAST KICK OF THE GAME, VIRTUALLY!
AND THAT'S IT! IT'S OVER! THERE'LL BE NO GIANT KILLING HERE TODAY.
HEY. THE STRIKER FOR MELCHESTER ROVERS.
SWAP?
I WOULD LIKE TO OWN THE SHIRT OF THE MAN WHO SCORED THAT GOAL.
UH...NO OFFENCE, BUT SO WOULD I.
I'M GOING TO GET THIS FRAMED FOR MY DAD.
THANK YOU, THOUGH.
I UNDERSTAND.
I WILL SEE YOU AGAIN, ROY RACE.
BE LUCKY.

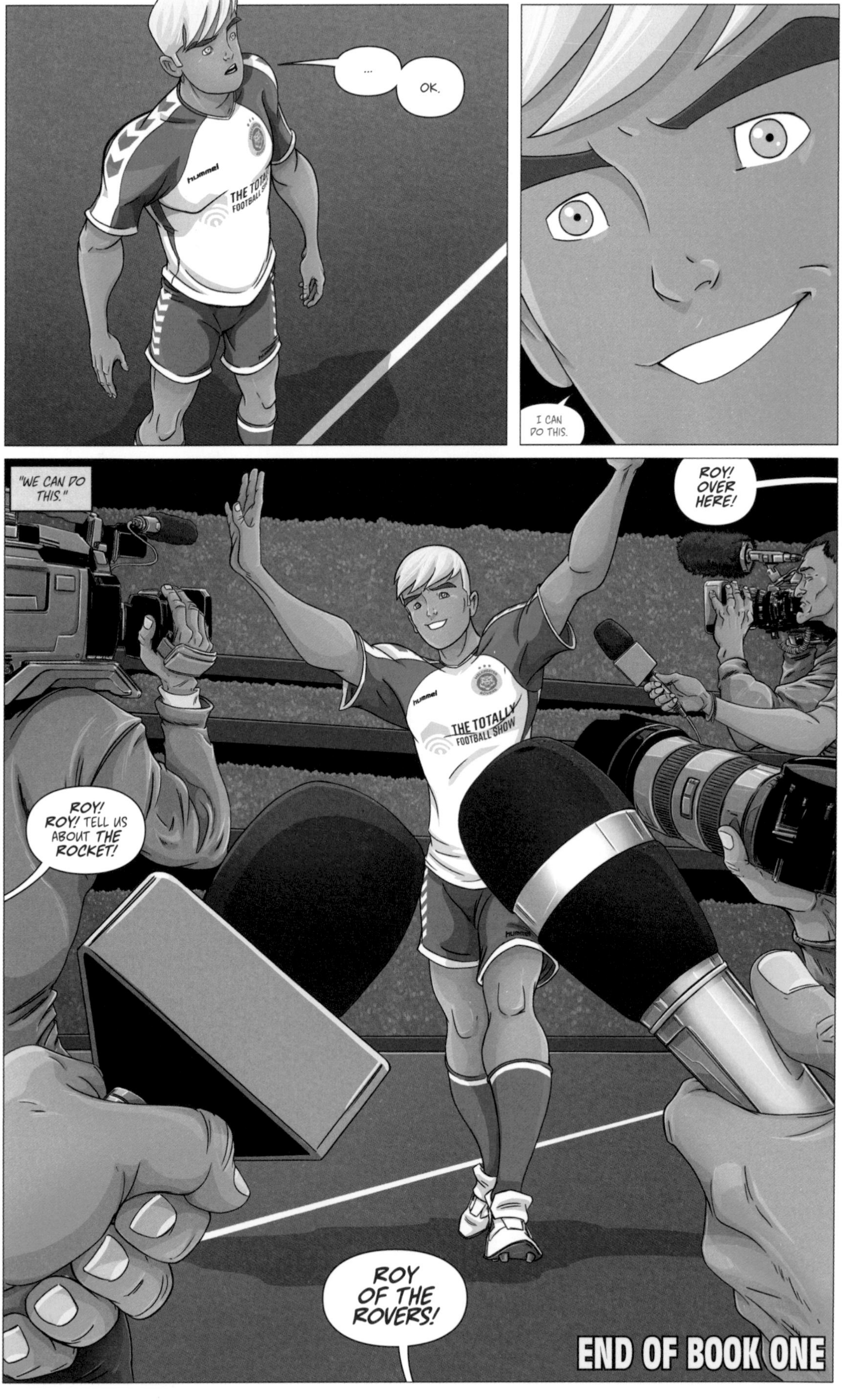
...
OK.
I CAN DO THIS.
"WE CAN DO THIS."
ROY! OVER HERE!
ROY! ROY! TELL US ABOUT THE ROCKET!
ROY OF THE ROVERS!
END OF BOOK ONE

MELCHESTER

ROVERS

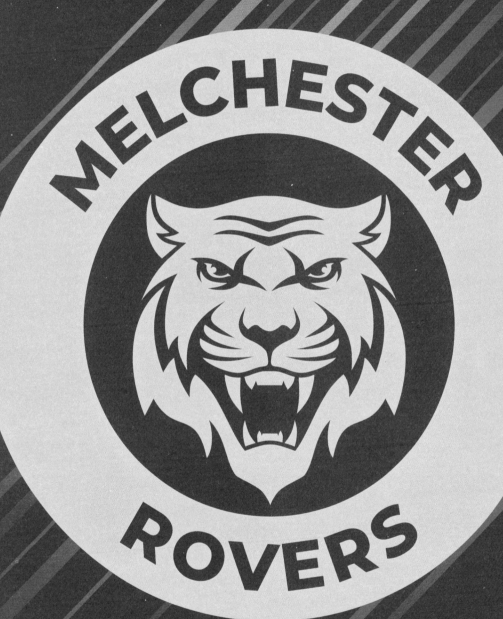

ROY OF THE ROVERS™

THE FIRST SEASON

Keep track of every new ***Roy of the Rovers*** book here!
Don't forget to tick the boxes as you read each one.

FICTION

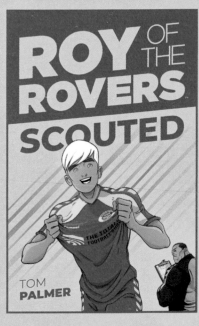

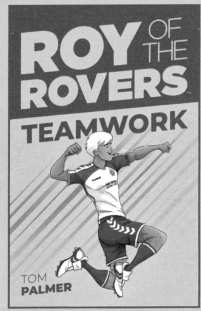

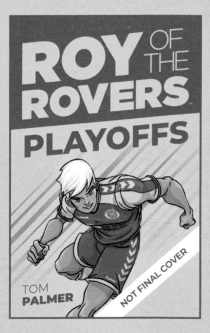

ROY OF THE ROVERS
SCOUTED
TOM
PALMER

BOOK 1
SCOUTED

Author: Tom Palmer
Out: October 2018
ISBN: 978-1-78108-698-8

Roy Race is the most talented striker in Melchester – but is he good enough to catch the eye of the Melchester Rovers scouts?

READ? ☐

ROY OF THE ROVERS
TEAMWORK
TOM
PALMER

BOOK 2
TEAMWORK

Author: Tom Palmer
Out: February 2019
ISBN: 978-1-78108-707-7

Life gets tricky for Roy as he adjusts to life in the spotlight. Fortune and glory await, but can Roy juggle football, fame and family?

READ? ☐

ROY OF THE ROVERS
PLAYOFFS
TOM
PALMER
NOT FINAL COVER

BOOK 3
PLAYOFFS

Author: Tom Palmer
Out: May 2019
ISBN: 978-1-78108-722-0

Crunch time for Rovers: the end of the season is here, the club is in deep trouble, and it's down to Roy to bring a bit of hope back to the Melchester faithful.

READ? ☐

GRAPHIC NOVELS

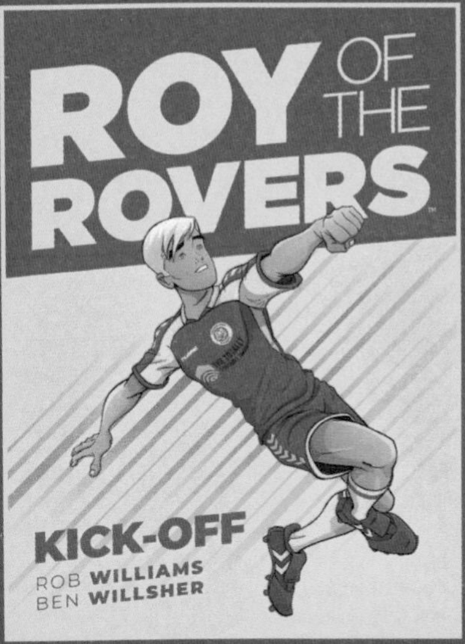
ROY OF THE ROVERS
KICK-OFF
ROB WILLIAMS
BEN WILLSHER

BOOK 1

KICK-OFF

Writer: Rob Williams
Artist: Ben Willsher
Out: November 2018
ISBN: 978-1-78108-652-0

Roy Race is 16, talented, and desperate to make it as a footballer. But is he good enough for Melchester Rovers? Now's the time to prove if he's got what it takes to become Roy of the Rovers.

READ? ☐

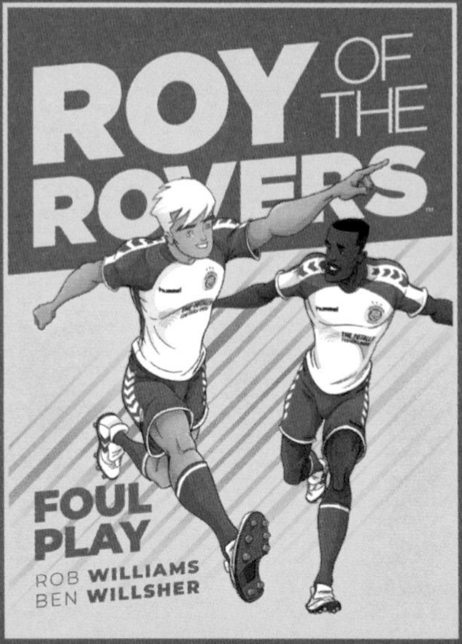
ROY OF THE ROVERS
FOUL PLAY
ROB WILLIAMS
BEN WILLSHER

BOOK 2

FOUL PLAY

Writer: Rob Williams
Artist: Ben Willsher
Out: March 2019
ISBN: 978-1-78108-669-8

Roy picks up an injury that puts him on the sidelines, and suddenly there's competition for his place as a brand new - and brilliant - striker is brought in by the management...

READ? ☐

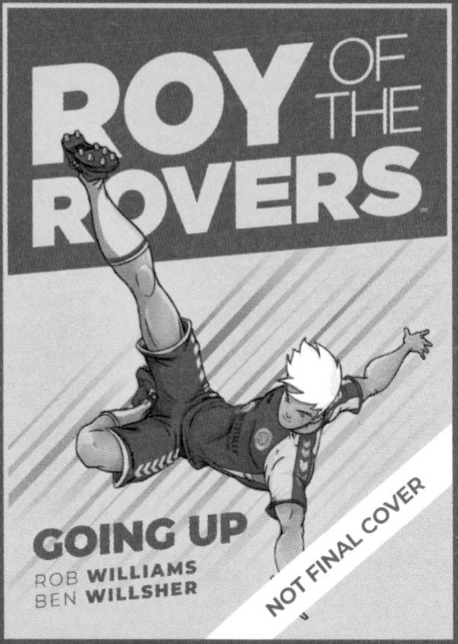
ROY OF THE ROVERS
GOING UP
ROB WILLIAMS
BEN WILLSHER
NOT FINAL COVER

BOOK 3

GOING UP

Writer: Rob Williams
Artist: Ben Willsher
Out: June 2019
ISBN: 978-1-78108-673-5

Roy and the team have battled through a tough season, but have they got enough left to get promoted? Or will they fall at the final hurdle and see the club sold by its greedy owner?

READ? ☐

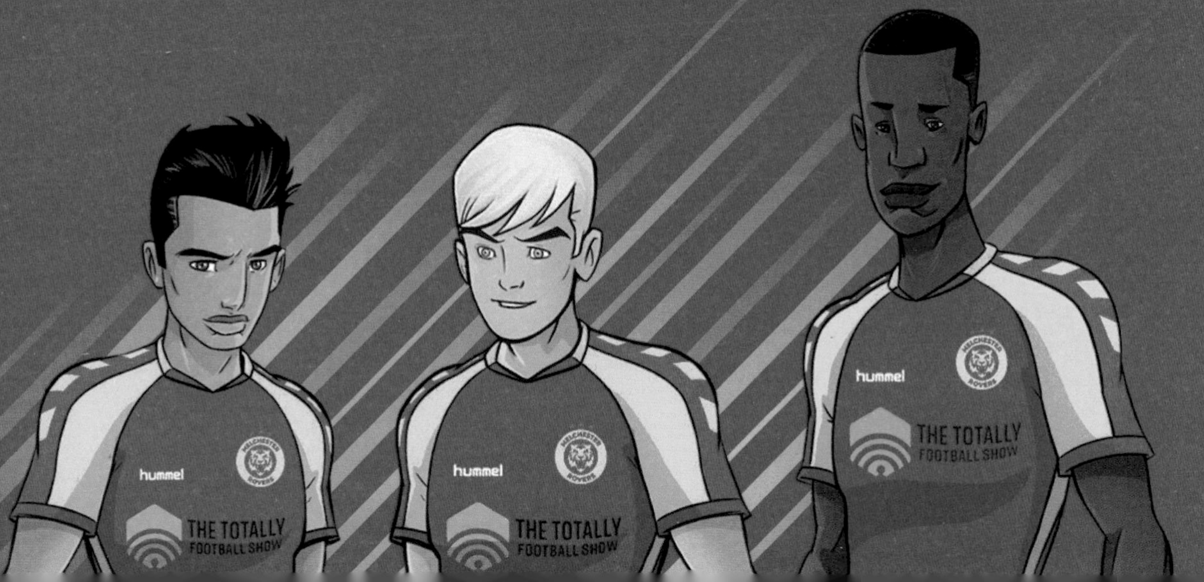
hummel
THE TOTALLY FOOTBALL SHOW
hummel
THE TOTALLY FOOTBALL SHOW
hummel
THE TOTALLY FOOTBALL SHOW

PLAYER INTERVIEW

Introduce yourself

Hi, I'm Roy Race. I'm the new Melchester Rovers striker!

Do you have a nickname?

At Melchester? Occasionally people call me Racey... same as at my old club Grimroyd.

Who was your favourite team growing up?

I'm playing for them! My family have supported the Rovers since, like, forever! My Dad is Melchester's biggest fan and knows literally everything about the club and its incredible history.

Who is the best player that you have played with?

So far, I couldn't pick one out of the Rovers side – they're all great. After trialling in goal for a bit though, I have a lot more respect for what Gordon Stewart has to do!

Who is the best player that you have played against?

Hugo is pretty spectacular. I felt for our defense whenever he was in possession of the ball during our cup game against Tynecaster. He really is a different class.

Do you have a pre-match routine?

Before home games, I like to have breakfast with my Mum, Dad and sister Rocky, whilst wearing my favourite Melchester Rovers top.

What's your advice to young players?

Wow! Well, I'm kind of still a young player myself, so I don't know really. I guess I would say never give up and keep on practising.

What's your favourite social media network and why?

Instagram is cool... I've seen some great football clips on Snapchat as well.

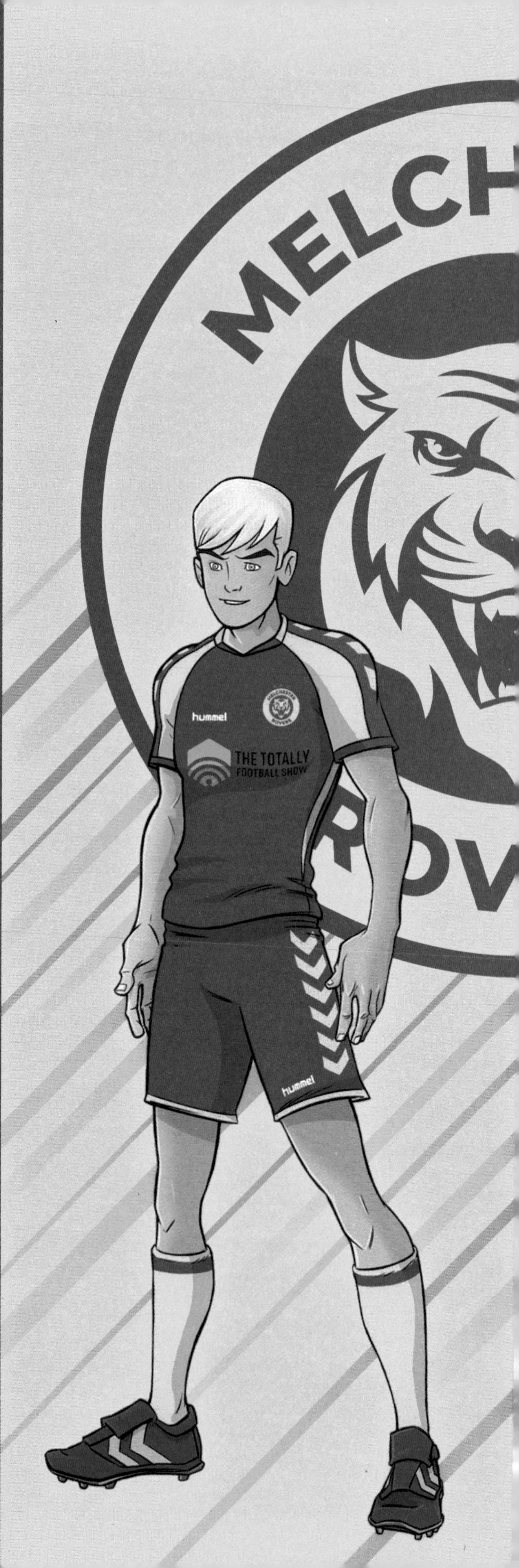
MELCH
ROV
hummel
THE TOTALLY
FOOTBALL SHOW
hummel

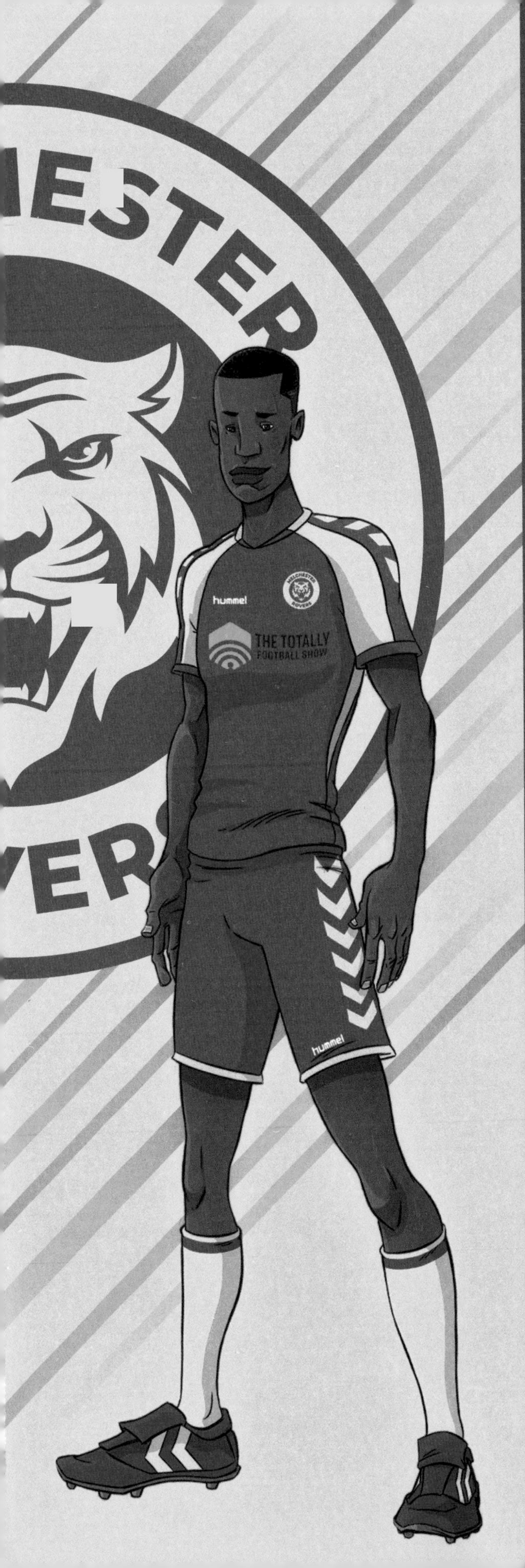
hummel
THE TOTALLY FOOTBALL SHOW
hummel

PLAYER INTERVIEW

Introduce yourself

Lofty Peak. Defender.

Do you have a nickname?

Yeah, Lofty.

So what is your real first name?

It's not Lofty!

Who was your favourite team growing up?

I'm a local, so Melchester Rovers. I'm also a big B-ball fan as well, so I should shout out to my boys the Melchester Swish.

Who is the best player that you have played with?

My boy, Roy Race. Have you seen him shoot with that left foot? Devastating man! We call it Racey's Rocket on the training ground...

Who is the best player that you have played against?

Ha! Hugo, no doubt. That guy made me tired man, he's quality.

Do you have a pre-match routine?

Nah, not really. I listen to some music... get in the zone a bit, y'know?

What's your advice to young players?

What, am I old now?!? I would say just keep playing. And remember to do some proper stretching exercises before starting a game. It's important to keep limber!

What's your favourite social media network and why?

Twitter – keep it short and sweet man!